BLACK CAT MYSTERY Magazine

VOL. 3, NO. 4 ISSUE #12

FEATURES

NEW STORIES

CLASSIC REPRINT

 Published by Wildside Press LLC, 9745 MacArthur Blvd, Suite 215, Cabin John, MD 20818 USA. Visit us online: wildsidepress.com | bcmystery.com.

FROM THE CAT'S PERCH

Mysteries come in an infinite variety of subgenres, and mystery writers will debate ad infinitum about the definitions of each of them. I am most often caught up in debates about the definition of noir, but when I sent out the submission call for this issue I found myself in discussions with several writers about what exactly defines a cozy, and what differentiates a cozy from a traditional mystery.

For this issue, here's the definition I settled on and which I asked writers to keep in mind as they wrote their stories: Cozies are a subgenre of crime fiction in which sex and violence occur off stage, the detective is an amateur sleuth, and the crime and detection take place in a small, socially intimate community.

Did all the writers agree with my definition? No, but the ten writers included in this issue—K.L. Abrahamson, N.M. Cedeño, Debra H. Goldstein, Darren Goossens, Gordon Linzner, Charlotte Morganti, Alan Orloff, Bev Vincent, Stacy Woodson, and Elizabeth Zelvin—each brought something special to their stories, and I'm certain you'll appreciate their individual takes on the cozy.

Also included is a blast from the past, a classic reprint selected by our publisher.

So sit back, relax, and take a walk on the mild side.

—Michael Bracken
Editor, *Black Cat Mystery Magazine*

Staff

PUBLISHER & EXECUTIVE EDITOR
John Gregory Betancourt

EDITOR
Michael Bracken

WILDSIDE PRESS SUBSCRIPTION SERVICES
Karl Würf

PRODUCTION TEAM
Sam Hogan
Karl Würf

YE OLDE PAWNE SHOPPE

ALAN ORLOFF

Staunton Wickersham hunched over the sales counter, reading a back issue of *American Chess Magazine* and petting Spassky, one of his two Persian cats, as the door to his chess store opened. In breezed Ballysburg's best baker, Betsy Brighton, owner of The Cupcake Cottage, carrying a plate of freshly-baked delicacies. "Good morning, Stan," she trilled, marching right up to the sales counter. She set the plate down on the glass and ran a hand through Spassky's thick black fur. "Hiya, Spazz! *Koochy-koochy-koo!* Aren't you just *purrrrr*-fect?"

The cat escaped her grasp and jumped down from the counter, off to find his running mate Fischer, most likely napping in the back.

Betsy was a full-figured gal, and she wore a low-cut dress under her pink cupcake-festooned apron. She leaned forward, and Staunton couldn't help but get an ample eyeful of her ample bosom.

"Brought you some goodies," Betsy said, displaying her wares.

"Yes, yes, I can see that."

Betsy leaned forward even farther, and for a second, Staunton imagined her toppling over the counter, smack into his lap. That scenario did not seem unpleasant.

"See anything that looks good?"

"Pardon?" Staunton said.

"See anything you want to just dive right into?"

Staunton remained mesmerized by Betsy's bounty. "Excuse me?"

Betsy tapped the plate of cupcakes with a red-shellacked fingernail. "Stan! Have a cupcake. They're delicious, if I do say so myself."

The mention of a delicious cupcake broke the hold Betsy's bosom had on Staunton. He smiled, plucked a chocolate-iced-with-rainbow-sprinkles number off the plate, and took a generous bite. Heavenly! It had to rank right up there with the best he'd ever tasted—Betsy was indeed a bodacious baker. "Delectable," he managed, mouth full.

Betsy beamed. "Where are all your chess buddies?"

"We take Wednesdays off." Most mornings, a few of Staunton's chess friends would play games on folding card tables set up in the rear of the store. Wednesday was the one day they'd all decided to set aside for running errands. After all, you couldn't play chess *every* day of the week.

"You know, Stan, when you speak to me with that charming British accent, it sounds like you're giving me a compliment. Like you're flirting with me."

Could Betsy read a person's intentions just from an accent? "I, uh, no, it's just that..."

Betsy blushed. "Thank you."

Staunton had been entertaining thoughts of asking Betsy out on a date for the past few weeks, and now the opportunity presented itself. But before he could take advantage of the moment, the store phone rang, and he answered it. "Ye Olde Pawne Shoppe, Staunton Wickersham, proprietor, speaking."

"Staunton, this is Officer Bishop. I'm afraid I've got some bad news. Hiram Knight is in the hospital with a knot on his head the size of a peach."

Good lord! "Will he be okay?"

"Docs say he'll be fine. He should be allowed visitors later today, if you want to swing by to check on him. Cheer him up."

"Do you know what happened?"

"Evidently, someone attacked him and stole a valuable chess set. He can't remember much about the details, though. Docs say his memory might—or might not—return. Anyway, he wanted me to call you and a few others."

Staunton couldn't believe his ears. Who would want to harm Hiram Knight? And what lowlife would steal a man's prized chess set?

"Staunton? You there?"

"Oh, yes, of course, Officer."

"Listen, if someone tries to sell you that set, or if you hear of someone trying to sell it to some other dealer, let me know, okay?"

"Sure thing." Staunton hung up and turned to Betsy, whose eyes had grown wide from hearing his side of the conversation. He repeated what Bishop had told him to fill in the gaps.

"Oh, my, that's terrible. Such a nice old man."

Knight wasn't much older than he or Betsy. "Yes, a true shame. I hope that Officer Bishop will catch the perpetrator."

Betsy scoffed. "I wouldn't pin your hopes on it. You know Bishop is a walking blunder. He just isn't up to the task, bless his heart. Why, he couldn't even beat me in a game of checkers if I spotted him three pieces and played with my eyes closed."

She had a point. Staunton's few dealings with Bishop had never resulted in a satisfactory outcome. He sighed. "You're probably right."

Betsy's face brightened. "That's why we need to help."

"We? Help?" Staunton recalled the old TV show *I Love Lucy*, where Lucy was always persuading poor Ethel to assist her in some hare-brained scheme. "I'm not so sure that sounds like a good idea."

"Pish posh. Who would know that a particular chess set was valuable? Valuable enough to *whonk* someone over the head for? And who would even know that Hiram *owned* such a chess set? I hate to say it, but that narrows things down. A lot. The thief must be local, and they're most likely a chess player. There's one person who knows all the local chess players. You." She pointed at Staunton's face dramatically. "Do any of your chess friends have it in for Hiram?"

"Preposterous. We've all been friends for years. No one would do that to Hiram." But Staunton had to admit, Betsy's logic made sense. Four of Staunton's closest chess-playing mates had been playing round robins and kibitzing together for over a decade: Noel Martin, Cara Ricci, Dom "The Fork" Davenport, along with Knight. Everyone in their little group knew that Staunton had just sold a fourteen thousand dollar set to Knight. But they were all his friends, weren't they?

Weren't they?

Betsy stood up straight and stuck her chest out, ready for battle. "Don't fret, Stan. You and I are going to solve the mystery. Hiram's your friend, right? He'd do the same for you, wouldn't he?"

Despite their friendship, Knight didn't seem like the mystery-solving sort. "I don't know."

Betsy's eyes twinkled. "How about if I bring over some more cupcakes to fortify us for the task?"

Sold.

* * * *

Staunton and Betsy had taken the replenished plate of cupcakes over to one of the empty card tables and were plotting their next moves, when Noel Martin burst through the door. "Hear about Hiram?"

"Yes, we heard. Terrible." Staunton pointed to a chair. "Have a seat. Betsy and I were just, ah, discussing it." They'd been making a list of possible suspects, and Noel's name was right near the top.

Noel sat and nodded at the plate of cupcakes. "Mind?"

"Help yourself," Betsy said.

Martin selected a maple glazed and scarfed down a few bites before speaking. When he did, the pain was plain on his face. "Terrible, just terrible. Who would do that to a person? Just for a chess set. No offense, Staunton. I know you sell them, and all, but..."

"It wasn't just any old chess set, was it?" Betsy said.

"No, it wasn't. It was an exquisite set, truly one-of-a-kind. But Hiram could have been killed."

Martin was spot on, it *was* an exquisite set, designed by the famed Italian artist Ferraducci. Staunton sold a set that valuable only a couple of times a year, if he was lucky. Intricately carved onyx pieces. Gold and silver inlaid board. An ornate matching chess clock. The entire sale ran upwards of fourteen thousand dollars. And it could have been higher, if Staunton had put the set up for auction. Because Knight wasn't the only one who had become obsessed with the set from the moment it had entered the shop. Martin also had wanted it and hadn't been very happy when Staunton sold it to Knight, solely because Knight had expressed interest first.

Staunton had just explained all that to Betsy right before Martin had come barging in.

"Didn't you want to buy that chess set, too?" Betsy put some honey in her voice.

"Well, sure. It's no secret I wanted it," Martin said as Fischer rubbed up against his leg, leaving a few white hairs on his pants. Noel shifted position, and Fischer moved with him, then Martin tried to shoo him away with one hand, but the kitty didn't take the hint. Martin finally gave up and lifted his head. "Surely you don't think I had something to do with this, do you? Hiram is one of my closest friends. I'm heartbroken."

Staunton shrugged. "Officer Bishop is doing his best to capture the thief. Maybe he'll be able to get some usable fingerprints and identify the culprit."

"Fingerprints? In Hiram's condo?"

"Where else?"

Martin's squirming intensified, and Spassky jumped down from his perch on the sales counter and meandered over to join Fischer. Together, the two cats sashayed figure eights around Martin's legs. Over the years, Staunton noticed how attuned his fluffies were to other people's emotional vibrations. "Well, I, uh…"

"What?"

"I went to see Hiram this morning. Early. To see if he wanted to go get coffee. And to…to…uh…" Martin's mouth slowly closed.

"Oh, for cake's sake, just spit it out," Betsy said.

"I also wanted to see if he'd consider selling me the Ferraducci."

"Really?"

"Yes. I offered him twenty percent more than he paid for it, but he declined." Noel gave a dry little chuckle. "Said he'd sell it to me for twice what he paid. I tried to negotiate with him, but he refused, saying I was trying to rook him. Got a little heated about it, too. Needless to say, we didn't get any coffee." Martin's eyes misted. "I swear, when I left, Hiram was fine. A little peeved, but fine."

"I don't suppose there were any witnesses to that," Betsy asked.

Martin sighed deeply. "Actually…"

Like pulling teeth, Staunton thought. "Actually what?"

"As I was pulling away in my car, I thought I saw The Fork walk into the building."

* * * *

Dom "The Fork" Davenport stretched the measuring tape to six feet six inches in bare feet, but only tipped the scales at one-fifty-five, no matter how much he forked into his mouth. Some thought his nickname came from that voracious appetite, but it really came from his love of forking his opponent's pieces on the chessboard. He now sat where Martin had been sitting half an hour ago, and he held a cupcake in each hand.

After the *hello-how-are-yous* were over—and Davenport's cupcakes devoured—Betsy got right down to business. "There was a witness who saw you going inside Hiram's condo building, just before he got his bean clobbered."

Davenport glanced from Betsy to Staunton and back to Betsy. "That's right. I did go to see him. But when I left, his bean was intact, I can assure you."

"No offense, Dom, but that's exactly what the assailant would say, you know," Betsy said.

"I expect that's true," Davenport said. "But I'd never do that to Hiram. To anybody. I can't even kill a fly that's gotten in the house. Ask Mildred if you don't believe me."

"Terrible thing, what happened," Staunton said. "And I know we all want to get to the bottom of it. So can you tell us why you went to see him? Maybe you saw something there that could identify who really did this?"

"Look, I'll do whatever I can to help Hiram. But if you could keep what we discuss here private, I'd appreciate it." He bent over and scratched Fischer on his head, who, miraculously didn't fuss.

"We'll do the best we can," Staunton said.

"Thank you." Davenport licked his lips, then continued. "I've been a little short the past six months, and I know Hiram bought that fancy set from you. Plus, he lives like a king, so I figured, he'd...he'd be able to lend me some money. Just until the beginning of the year. Then I'd pay him back, with a little interest, too."

"Hey, it happens to all of us," Staunton said. If his online business hadn't increased since that Netflix chess show had spurred interest in the sport, he'd be struggling to make the rent himself.

"Nothing to be ashamed of," Betsy added.

"Well, I'm *not* proud of it. I seem to have miscalculated the revenues for my rental property. And I wasn't expecting to have to replace the washer and dryer. Anyway, Hiram turned me down. I guess I'll just have to tighten my belt even farther. I'm used to making a sacrifice." Davenport seemed resigned to the fact that his financial woes would continue.

Knight's refusal surprised Staunton. Knight was usually very generous to his friends, and he *had* been spending more money on chess sets the past eighteen months. In addition to the Ferraducci, Staunton had sold him two other four-figure sets in that timeframe.

Of course, the fact that Davenport had the motive, the means, and the opportunity made him a prime suspect. But would he have admitted going to Knight for a loan if he'd then stolen the set? Most folks, no, but Davenport was a wily chess player, and masters planned their moves well in advance.

"How long were you there at Hiram's?" Betty asked.

"'Bout fifteen minutes."

"Describe what you saw. From the beginning."

"Okay, sure. I knocked at the door and he told me to come on in," Davenport said. "So I did, and there he was. Just sitting at his chess table staring at a game laid out on his fancy set. You know how Hiram gets when he's contemplating his next move. Still as a statue. Barely acknowledged me. After about a minute, he looked up. Said hello."

"Then what?" Betsy asked. Spassky had hopped up onto the sales counter where he could have a good look at the goings-on. And the remaining cupcakes.

"Then I explained my situation. When I was done, he apologized, but said he was a little strapped himself, couldn't give me the loan. He said he felt bad saying no, and I felt bad hearing no. I left shortly after that."

"See anybody else on your way out?"

"Nope." Davenport shook his head somberly, then stopped in mid-shake. "There was one other thing, now that I remember. Hiram got a phone call while I was there. He answered it, turned his back and mumbled a few words, then hung up."

"Any idea who called?"

"Well…" Davenport's face flushed.

"What?" Staunton said.

"Well, it sounded like Cara. I couldn't be sure, but I thought I heard Hiram invite her over. And after the call, he had a little extra pep in his step."

* * * *

Cara Ricci owned Cara's Candle Country, a boutique across Main Street from Staunton's chess store. Every time Staunton stepped foot in her shop, he was overwhelmed by the scents: cinnamon, lavender, vanilla, and whatever the heck potpourri was. After spending just a few minutes in the store, it all just smelled like wax to him.

Now, he and Betsy sat on a comfy loveseat in the back of her shop, while Cara sunk into an overstuffed armchair, cup of tea cradled in her hand. She had curly brown hair and engaging brown eyes, and sat with the bearing of a queen. Staunton could see why Knight might have had a thing for her.

"Would you two like some tea?" Cara asked.

Staunton considered accepting, but he was sure to be disappointed. After all these years living in the States, he still hadn't gotten accustomed to what many Americans tried to pass off as tea. "Thank you, but no."

"None for me, either." Betsy handed Cara a small white bakery box, tied with white string. Inside were two carrot cake cupcakes. "Here's a treat for later."

"Thank you." Cara took a precise sip of tea, then lowered her cup. "I'm really angry about what happened to Hiram. He's such a nice man."

"Yes, he is," Staunton said. "That's what has me so perplexed. Who would want to do that to him?"

"Probably some deranged lunatic," Cara said.

"We don't think so. In fact," Betsy said, leaning in for effect. When she'd gone back to her shop for more cupcakes earlier, she'd changed into a blouse that covered more of her decolletage. "We think it was someone he knew. A friend of his, perhaps. Who else would know he owned that expensive chess set?"

Cara seemed to ponder that for a moment. "Then that's even worse."

Staunton hesitated, not sure how to proceed. While he was thinking, Betsy charged ahead. "Is it true that you went to visit Hiram? Right before he was *shnocked* on the head?"

"Why, I…" She straightened. "Yes. Yes I did drop in on him. We had a brief discussion, and then I left. He was, as you might say, un*shnocked* when I left."

"What was your discussion about?" Staunton asked.

"I'm sure you heard. Everyone in the chess community seems to have heard."

Staunton *had* heard some scuttlebutt about Cara accusing Knight of cheating in a recent match they had at a regional tourney. However, he hadn't had a chance to discuss the incident with Knight to see what the real story was. Staunton simply nodded, *go on.*

"Well, I was playing Hiram in the semi-finals at Wattleboro, and I swear he was getting signals from one of the onlookers. He opened with the Budapest Gambit, and then—you know how inconsistent this is with Hiram's style—he tried to spring the Fajarowicz Trap on me. I thwarted him of course, but he seemed to get advice along the way from his accomplice. He ended up winning and punching his ticket to the state tourney."

"That sounds, well, highly unusual, especially for Hiram."

"Exactly. Anyway, I went to confront him about it. He denied everything, of course. In fact…" Cara blushed, and then took a sip of tea, trying to hide her embarrassment.

"What?" Betsy asked.

"Nothing."

"He asked you out, didn't he?" Betsy said.

Cara's eyes went wide, and Staunton wasn't sure if it was because of the audacity of Betsy's guess, or because she'd nailed it.

Staunton interposed, trying to ease the tension. "I don't think that Betsy means to—"

Cara waved a hand in the air. "Oh, a woman always knows, right? Yes, he asked me out. Said he'd had feelings for me for a long time."

"What did you say?" Betsy asked.

"I politely declined. And I told him that I was seeing someone else."

"You have a boyfriend?" Staunton asked. This was the first he'd heard about it.

Cara met his eyes. "Yes. Noel and I have started seeing each other. We're really quite in love."

Staunton's mind raced. Cara and Noel Martin? Really? And he hadn't noticed a thing? Maybe he needed to get his nose out of all the chess magazines once in a while and observe his surroundings.

"And what was Hiram's reaction when you told him this?" Betsy asked.

"He wasn't a happy camper."

* * * *

Lying in his hospital bed, Knight didn't look too bad to Staunton—if you ignored the white bandage covering his entire scalp. He was sitting up, drinking from one of those flimsy plastic pitchers through a straw, and every time he took a sip, the pitcher seemed ready to jiggle out of his hand and dump into his lap. Staunton held his breath, bracing for water to slosh everywhere.

Betsy had wanted to come along, but Staunton wasn't sure what kind of mood Knight would be in. Getting *clonked* on the noggin was apt to put people in a sour one.

"How are you feeling?" Staunton asked.

"Okay, considering," said Knight, a little hoarse. He set the pitcher down and Staunton exhaled a sigh of relief.

"And you have no idea who did this to you?"

"Not a one," Knight answered, keeping his head completely still, as if the slightest movement would cause him pain.

"Well, with any luck, your memory will come back to you."

"Yeah. Although part of me wants to forget the whole thing and move on."

"But the thief got your Ferraducci."

"I know. It was a beauty, all right. But it was insured. I can always buy another set. Although, if thieves are going to keep coming after them…"

Staunton felt for his friend. He knew how much that set had meant to Knight. "If there's anything I can do for you, just let me know."

"I didn't think I'd have to stay overnight, so will you do me a favor? Will you feed Catsparov?"

"Certainly."

"Great. My keys are in my pants, in the closet. Be sure to lock up when you leave. Wouldn't want anyone to break in and take something."

* * * *

Staunton picked Betsy up on the way to Knight's condo. On the short drive over, they discussed what they'd learned.

"Any of them could have done it—they all seemed to have a motive. Noel wanted the Ferraducci set, so he offered to buy it at a premium from Hiram. After Hiram turned him down, maybe he came back, *thwacked* Hiram on the skull and stole the set."

"I don't know. If he did, where would he keep it? He couldn't display it on the chance we'd see it. That's half the pleasure of owning a set like that," Staunton said.

"Perhaps. But then there's Dom. Hiram didn't give him the loan, so maybe Dom snuck back, trying to outflank him, and mashed Hiram's melon, then stole the set, aiming to sell it for his needed cash."

Staunton shook his head. "Not really Dom's style. He's more of a lover than a fighter. He's as docile as a kitten."

"Well, then, how about Cara? She's convinced Hiram cheated her out of a trip to the state tourney. Maybe she smashed his pumpkin so that he'd have to withdraw, and she could take his place?"

"Cara doesn't strike me as the smashing pumpkin type. Besides, I think I read somewhere that candle lovers are all pacifists." Staunton pulled into a spot in Knight's parking lot. "Let's go feed Catsparov. And while we're there, maybe we should look around a bit, just in case Officer Bishop missed something."

When Staunton got up to Knight's apartment, there was no indication that a crime had been committed. No stretch of yellow crime scene tape. No fingerprint dust. No chalk outline on the floor.

Betsy noticed it, too. "Everything looks neat and tidy. No sign of a struggle or anything."

Did Staunton detect just a bit of disappointment in Betsy's tone?

"How about if you feed the cat, while I nose around?"

Betsy's face sagged.

"Don't worry, after you're done, you can snoop around, too."

She brightened. "Deal."

She went into the kitchen and Staunton entered the main living area. To his right was a large shelving unit that displayed a number of Knight's more interesting—and valuable—chess sets, along with a bunch of chess books stacked in a column. In the middle of the room was the small square chess table, now empty save for the remnants of a meal: a plate still holding a half-eaten sandwich, a glass of soda, and an economy-sized bag of chips. Evidently, Knight had been attacked right in the middle of lunch.

Staunton stood there, observing, pondering, cogitating.

The sound of a can opener broke his concentration, and a moment later, Catsparov emerged from the bedroom, beelining straight for the kitchen. *Koochy-koochy* sounds greeted the Abyssinian as he entered the kitchen.

The *koochies* stopped shortly thereafter, and Betsy joined Staunton by the chess table. "Find any clues? Draw any conclusions?"

"As a matter of fact," Staunton said, "I did."

* * * *

On the way back to the hospital, Staunton called Officer Bishop. "Did you move anything in Knight's condo when you were there?"

"No, we left everything just the way it was. Took pictures of the place, too, as we processed the scene. Why are you asking?"

"If you can meet us at the hospital, I'll explain everything. I just need to ask Hiram a few questions first." Staunton hung up.

"What was that all about? You know what happened, don't you?"

Staunton suppressed a smile. "I believe I do."

On the drive over, Betsy tried to pry it out of Staunton, but he didn't concede.

When they reached Knight's room, he was in the same position Staunton had left him in—sitting up, head bandaged. He muted the TV as they entered. "Feed Catsparov? How is my little buddy?"

"He's su-*purrrr*," Betsy said. "What a great little fella."

"He is, isn't he?" Knight nodded to the closet. "If you wouldn't mind putting the keys back in my pants pocket, I'd appreciate it."

Staunton did as requested, then returned to Knight's bedside. Betsy crowded in next to him. "Any memory of the incident come back yet?"

"Nope. Not yet."

"When I was in your apartment, I noticed that you were in the middle of a meal when you got attacked."

"If you say so."

"There was part of a sandwich on a plate," Staunton said.

"Ham and Swiss? That's what I usually have for lunch."

"I believe it was." Staunton paused. "It was on your chess table, along with a drink and big bag of chips."

Knight tilted his head quizzically. "Okay…"

"It was on your chess table, where you always keep the Ferraducci."

Knight closed one eye, stared at Staunton. "And?"

"*And* if you were eating lunch on the chess table, that would mean that the set could *not* have been on the table—it's much too small to hold your food *and* the chess set. Which meant that you were eating lunch *after* the chess set had been removed."

Knight's eyes narrowed. "You mean stolen."

"No, I mean *removed*, Hiram. I believe you staged the whole charade. You packed up the set and hid it someplace, in the back of a closet or maybe the trunk of your car. Then you struck yourself on the head and called the police. Probably planned to collect the insurance money and then sell the set on the black market. Dom indicated that you might be having money troubles," Staunton said. "Must have hurt, whacking yourself like that."

"I did no such thing."

"Really? You're claiming that a thief—who happened to know you collect expensive chess sets—came into your apartment and took the Ferraducci, but left all the other valuable sets on the nearby shelves? And *then* you decided to have some lunch after getting clobbered on the head?"

Knight stared at Staunton for the longest time. "Sheesh, I never could get one past you, Staunton. I guess it's checkmate. Well played, sir. Well played."

* * * *

Officer Bishop arrived a few minutes later, and Knight admitted what Staunton had deduced, namely that he'd staged the whole thing. Staunton hoped that Knight's penalty wouldn't be too severe; he knew that money pressures sometimes made ordinarily good people commit desperate deeds.

"Why don't we celebrate?" Betsy said. "Come over to my place, and I'll whip up something delicious for dinner. And for dessert? I'll serve you a treat that will knock your socks off. And after that, we can have cupcakes!"

Staunton smiled. "Sounds simply splendid."

✗

Alan Orloff (www.alanorloff.com) has won two ITW Thriller Awards, including one for his story "Rent Due" (*Mickey Finn: 21st Century Noir*). He's also won a Derringer Award, been a finalist for the Shamus and Agatha Awards, and had a story selected for *The Best American Mystery Stories*. His latest novel is *I Play One On TV* from Down & Out Books.

THE GIRLS IN CABIN THREE

DEBRA H. GOLDSTEIN

Sunday

Dear Mom and Dad,

First night of camp. They won't let us into the dining room unless I write you a letter. So, here it is. I think they want a letter instead of a postcard to take up more time. Ms. Mott, the camp director, obviously realizes that after six years of being campers, our cabin knows how to dash off two-word postcards.

It's raining and there isn't much to do. The road to the dining room is muddy, but our cabin doesn't leak this year. They moved us to Cabin Three and told us to tell you to put that on our mail. We have new counselors. Their names are Eve and Mary. Eve looks like she could play football. Mary seems nicer.

Five of us are back from last year and we have one new girl in our cabin. I got a top bunk. Carolyn grabbed the one across from me. Yay! Kimi is under her. Like always, she smiles all the time. Her aunt took her to get the neatest cornrows before camp. Unlike Carolyn's wispy hair, Kimi says my thick mop will be perfect for her to do a simple braid.

You remember Iris and Sue, the Jersey twins you met last year? They picked the bunk across the room. The new girl, Denise, got here last. She wanted me to move to the bottom. No way! She's also not thrilled that we've been coming to camp so long that Sweetie Pie, the camp cat, seems to have remembered us. She adopted our cabin as her home this summer. None of us, except Denise who swears she has pet allergies, wants the cat kicked out by the counselors, so the twins are keeping Sweetie Pie on their side of the room. This is long enough to get into dinner.

Love and Kisses,
Sharon

Tuesday

Mom and Dad,

Still raining. We're spending a lot of time in the cabin or dining room. The counselors say it will be better when it stops raining, and to kick off this week's skits, they got up and sang a stupid song at last night's dinner. All I know is it had a line about some guy named Joe Spivy and poison ivy and another one about Leonard Skinner getting something like potato main poisoning after dinner. After the poison ivy Carolyn and I got into our first year of camp, you better believe that isn't going to happen to us again. I guess we'll have to stop eating the mashed potatoes.

Sharon

Wednesday

Dear Mom,

I was going to send you and Dad a Polaroid picture of all of us, but—don't get mad and don't tell Dad—I don't know where the new camera he bought me is. I took some pictures and I thought I put it in my cubby, but I can't find it. We're all going to look for it tonight after we work on our skit. The Jersey twins came up with a great idea for a murder plot and I'm writing it. Gotta run—lunch.

Love,

S—

PS if I don't find my camera, I'll pay Dad back out of my allowance or set up a lemonade stand.

Thursday

Mom and Dad,

More rain. We can't do anything outside so Ms. Mott sent indoor activity kits to every cabin. I guess she decided we're too old to make braided bracelets because our cabin got a card magic set. Mary only has a few tricks up her sleeve, but Eve is really into it. She even smiled. Boring!

Carolyn, Kimi, and I worked on our murder skit instead. I was going to be the dead body (we took catsup packets from the dining room to make a sponge bag for blood), but we decided it would be funnier to kill a counselor than a camper.

Eve said no way. She can be so-o-oh grumpy. Mary agreed to do it. We were going to make her a pool counselor so all she'd have to wear is her bathing suit and gold whistle, but she said her whistle disappeared. Instead, she's wearing shorts, a T-shirt, and a smock. She'll carry paintbrushes like an arts and crafts counselor. The real arts and crafts counselor promised to help us make props today.

I'm going to be the detective—like Sherlock Holmes (if you open this before daddy gets home, thank him for reading me that book)—and Carolyn is going to be my Watson. Kimi, the twins, and Denise are going to be witnesses and the murderer. I'm not sure which one will be the killer or if I'll make the twins identical killers, but since I'm writing the skit, I'll figure it out by Sunday night.

XOXO

Sharon

Saturday

Mom and Dad,

It stopped raining!!!!!! Some kids went hiking, some swimming, but not us.

Mom and Dad, so many things went wrong. First, we were late getting out of the cabin for activities today because instead of making her bed for Ms. Mott's inspection, Denise had a hissy fit that someone took her favorite ring. I saw her wearing it yesterday. It's a lot like the one you gave me when I was ten. You know, a gold band with a pearl on it.

Denise swore she took it off and left it in the cabin when she went to take a shower and it was gone when she got back. Eve, Mary, and Ms. Mott searched the cabin, but no ring (and we didn't find my camera, either).

When Ms. Mott found out about my camera and Mary's whistle, she was upset with Eve and Mary for not having reported our missing things. She grounded all of us "until one of you admits what you did or tells me who took the missing items."

"That's not fair," I said, speaking for everyone as we stared at Denise. "We're not going to fink on each other."

Ms. Mott ignored me, but Mary saved the day. "Maybe instead of making the girls stay in the cabin, Eve and I can take them to the dining room for lunch and then, rather than swimming or hiking, we can practice our skit for tonight." She gave Ms. Mott the funniest sideway glance. "You know, it's the only place at camp that has a stage. We have to rehearse, so if we're in the dining room, no one can write their parents that on the first day without rain they were kept indoors as a punishment for something someone else did."

Before Ms. Mott answered, Denise sat on her unmade bunk, crossed her arms, and pouted. She's such a baby. "I should be allowed to go swimming. It's my ring that's missing. I'm going to tell my father!"

We all glared at her and Ms. Mott looked at Eve, who simply shrugged. "Not another word. All of you will go to the dining room for lunch and stay there practicing your skit. I'll be in my office if one of you wants to talk to me about the missing items."

Even if we knew who took Denise's stupid ring, none of us are going to tell, so we trooped over to the dining room. Denise kept giving Kimi and me the evil eye, probably because we shortsheeted her bed the other night. After lunch, on top of having to stay in the dining room, Ms. Mott made our cabin do KP duty. We had to clear all the trays and sponge them down before we could practice, as well as refill the condiments on every table. Mom, the food after lunch looked even worse than it did before we ate.

We finally got to practice. I gave everyone the props that the arts and crafts counselor helped us make yesterday. Everything was going fine until the part where Carolyn, knife in hand, pushed Mary (I gave Carolyn a bigger part and made the twins my Watsons). Mary was supposed to fall to the ground, stabbed by the aluminum-foil knife Kimi made. Instead, Mary grabbed her side and half jumped and half fell off the stage.

I thought she was giving an award-winning performance. The twins agreed because they applauded, but instead of jumping up and taking a bow, Mary lay on the floor and groaned. That's when I saw that the silver knife sticking up through her bloody fingers was real.

Denise screamed and we all ran toward Mary. Eve reached her first. "Sharon, get Ms. Mott and the rest of you stand in the middle of the room."

When Ms. Mott and I got back to the dining room, Eve was holding Mary's head in her lap. Ms. Mott ran to the phone on the wall and called 911. Then, she called the camp nurse.

The paramedics and our nurse came quickly. When they started to examine Mary, her hands still streaked with red, Ms. Mott sent us back to our cabin.

It was horrible. Everyone was upset. Kimi was crying and repeating the knife she gave Carolyn was make-believe. Carolyn was trying to calm her down by assuring her the knife she thrust at Mary was fake. The twins were real quiet, but I could tell they were shook, too. And Denise was Denise. She pouted.

Ms. Mott came to our cabin a little later. "Mary is going to be okay. It's what they call a flesh wound. She didn't even have to go to the hospital, but we're going to let her stay in the infirmary tonight."

"But all that blood?" Carolyn said.

"Catsup. Sharon, I understand one of the props you made in arts and crafts was a blood sponge."

"Yes, but I didn't get it right. There were sponges in the arts and crafts cabin, but no Saran Wrap. I got a piece from the dining hall while we were doing KP today to make one for tonight." I pulled the clear plastic wrap I'd taken out of my pocket.

Ms. Mott frowned. "Mary will come back to see you tomorrow when she picks up her possessions to go home."

One of the twins asked, "Why is Mary going home?"

"Her time at camp is over." Ms. Mott turned her gaze toward Eve. "Eve, I'd like to talk to you for a moment."

Ms. Mott took Eve into the portion of the cabin reserved for the counselors. It wasn't like we couldn't hear what was being said. You know how flimsy that partition between our bunks and the counselors' area is. I hushed everyone and we listened.

"Eve, Mary told me she saw the missing items in your duffel bag and confronted you about them. She thinks you used a slight of the hand trick to exchange the fake knife for a real one."

"I don't know what you're talking about."

"Let me see your duffel."

"And if I refuse?"

"We'll have to get the police out here. But, if I search your bag and we find the missing things, we can simply return the items and I'll let you go home, too."

"With everyone thinking I'm a thief?"

"We'll simply say the incident with Mary was traumatizing."

I heard a thump, which I guess was Eve pulling her bag down from the shelf and handing it to Ms. Mott. Everything was quiet for a few minutes. When she spoke, Eve didn't even try to keep her voice down. "I don't know how those things got in there. I didn't put them there and I didn't hurt Mary."

"We'll see about that," Ms. Mott said. "I'll get someone in here to watch the cabin, but then you're going to need to come with me."

I may not like Eve, but I remembered what Daddy and you taught me about standing up for what's right. I stuck my head around the partition and told Ms. Mott that Eve might not be a perfect counselor (I know Mom, if I can't say something nice, I shouldn't say anything at all, but I wanted to tell the whole truth), but she didn't take anything.

"Sharon, this isn't about you. Go back with the other girls."

"No, ma'am." I rushed to keep talking before she could say anything. "You need to check the garbage the paramedics threw out in the dining room. If you hurry, I'm sure you'll find the fake knife."

"What are you talking about?"

"Mary and I were going to tape a catsup-soaked sponge wrapped in Saran Wrap under her smock for tonight's performance. When Carolyn stabbed her by sliding the fake knife between Mary's arm and her body, Mary would press the Saran Wrap, it would pop open, and the audience would see blood. While we campers were cleaning the tables and refilling the condiments, Mary probably made a makeshift blood sponge with one of the kitchen sponges, Saran Wrap, and catsup."

"That seems a little far-fetched."

"Not really. When Eve and Mary were doing card tricks with us the other day, Mary was good at slipping things up her sleeve. I bet instead of up her sleeve, she put a real knife and a blood sponge under her shirt. When Carolyn stabbed her, Mary distracted us by stumbling and falling. At that moment, she pushed the blood pack, cut herself slightly with the real knife, and palmed the fake knife under her shirt."

Ms. Mott hesitated. I guess she was thinking through the possibility of what I'd said.

"I know I'm right and that Mary did it because she's the only one who could have been taking our things. Except for Denise, the rest of us know everything about each other. I don't know when Mary hid those things in Eve's duffel bag, but you can prove what I'm saying if you follow up now."

I was right. Ms. Mott found the aluminum-foil knife scrunched up in the trash with the paramedics' gloves and the wrapping from the bandage they put on Mary. She confronted Mary with the knife, and she confessed.

We're getting a new counselor for the rest of the summer and Ms. Mott offered me a counselor-in-training position for next year. I hope she assigns me the girls in Cabin Three.

Must run.... The sun is still out.

Love,
Sharon

Judge Debra H. Goldstein (www.DebraHGoldstein.com) writes Kensington's Sarah Blair mystery series (*Four Cuts Too Many, Three Treats Too Many, Two Bites Too Many,* and *One Taste Too Many*). Her short stories, which have been named Agatha, Anthony, and Derringer finalists, have appeared in numerous periodicals and anthologies including *Alfred Hitchcock's Mystery Magazine, Black Cat Mystery Magazine, Mystery Weekly, Malice Domestic Murder Most Edible, Masthead,* and *Jukes & Tonks.* Debra has served on the national boards of Sisters in Crime and Mystery Writers of America and been president of the Guppy and SEMWA chapters.

LAZY DAYS PARADE TAKES A TRAGIC TURN

CHARLOTTE MORGANTI

Some towns are famous for their antique shops, some for quilts, some for maple sugar pie. Over the last four years, my hometown of Blossom City has developed a reputation for its annual Lazy Days Parade. Not because it rivals the grandeur of the Rose Parade, but because of unexpected mishaps.

Except for a few adjustments because of the pandemic, this year's parade followed the usual format. And, as we townspeople have come to expect, something unexpected occurred.

Nigel Mallard, our mayor, died. Mid-parade. However, this was no mere mishap. It was murder.

Nigel's death rocked the town, especially the chair of the Lazy Days Festival planning committee. "Can you believe it, Persimmon?" Holly said when she phoned me a few days later. "I'm not sure how the fair will survive. It won't be easy to find another platinum sponsor. We may need to hold bake sales to fundraise."

I hated kicking friends when they were down so resisted mentioning that a town of thirty-four hundred could support only so many bake sales. Especially when the competition was the elementary school soccer team and their very determined mothers.

"On top of that," Holly said, "Nigel's death means we need a new parade organizer. Can you recommend anyone creative?"

"So not a Nigel clone, then?"

Holly giggled. "Exactly. Nigel Mallard couldn't think past his own name. I'm so done with parades built around ducks."

Nigel had organized the Lazy Days parades for the past four years. Right from the beginning of his reign, our parades produced unexpected mishaps with amazing regularity. Take, for example, the Blossom City Trumpet's headline the day following Nigel's first parade as grand pooh-bah:

Spectators Splatted at Lazy Days Parade

Mayor Mallard's inaugural duck-themed parade took place in 2017. It travelled the usual route along the north half of Main Street, through the fifty-foot, poorly lit Blossom Creek tunnel, and finally once more into daylight for the final stretch along South Main Street. At the head of the parade, a feather-caped Nigel rode aboard a motorized float made to resemble a mallard drake. I speculated that the unfortunate driver of the Mallardmobile, who was secreted inside the unventilated float, must have been either desperate for work or someone who never heard the word "claustrophobia." The Mallardmobile towed a trailer holding fifty live ducks contained within a large chicken-wire enclosure. In keeping with the "everything duck" motif, the local hunt club and their dogs followed the trailer. Confident their dogs were so fixated on the caged ducks that they wouldn't stray, the hunt club eschewed leashes.

Unfortunately, Joshua Vine, the pastor of the church situated on South Main Street, had not subscribed to Mayor Mallard's "Buy a pothole, fill a pothole" street maintenance plan. Therefore, the section of South Main Street just after the tunnel exit and fronting the church remained a tire-popping, axle-jarring roadway.

When the Mallardmobile and its trailer exited Blossom Creek Tunnel, Nigel fanned his feather cape and waved at the spectators on the sidewalk. Several wheelchair-bound residents of the Golden Homestead who were stationed in front of the church shook their arthritic fists in response to Nigel's waves. Ninety-year-old Henry Jones, no doubt speaking for the Homesteader victims of Nigel's sure-fire, can't-miss investment disasters, jeered. "Prince Ponzi. Pocket-picker."

At that moment, the trailer's right front wheel lurched through a deep pothole. The trailer rocked, unnerving its fowl passengers. The quacking and wing flapping almost obscured the crack of the rear wheel as it smacked into the crater and snapped from its axle. The trailer tipped onto its side, the chicken-wire lid of the enclosure came loose, fifty anxious ducks spilled onto South Main Street, and a dozen hunt dogs sprang into action.

The result was not surprising: men hollering, dogs baying, birds squawking, wings flapping. And poop splatting.

When the dust and feathers settled, Nigel announced to all the Homesteaders attempting to rid their lap blankets of the ducks' discharge: "You can blame Skinflint Vine for this debacle. He refused to kick in a few dollars for highway maintenance."

Pastor Vine's face purpled. "Hah! You mean highway robbery, Mallard. If I wasn't a man of peace, I'd put a few potholes in your head."

Duckies Shredded and Dyed at 2018 Lazy Days Parade

The following year Nigel banned dogs from the parade and opted for duck-costumed human marchers. Nigel's Lucky Duckies, a gaggle of children and small adults wearing flimsy paper duckling costumes, preceded the Mallardmobile along the parade route. A few dozen of Mallard's Fowl Flock, adults decked out in paper drake costumes, waddled behind the float.

The one-minute hailstorm erupted about the same time as the last of the Fowl Flock exited Blossom Creek Tunnel. Sixty seconds. Ample time for hail to shred the ducklings' costumes, for green and yellow costume dye to stain the marchers' skin, and for the downpour to drench the Golden Homesteaders as their wheelchairs laid rubber in a futile race for cover. Henry Jones, now ninety-one and still the oldsters' spokesperson, said, "That malevolent Mallard is giving mayors and ducks a bad name by targeting seniors. First, he takes our savings, then he splats us with excrement and now, this year, hail. Our lives would be better without him."

Even though Henry's aged avengers blamed Nigel for the storm, everyone applauded Nigel's decision to hire Ivy Jinks to make the costumes for future parades. After three decades of supplying Blossom City with hand-tailored clothing, Ivy definitely knew the meaning of "color-fast."

Ivy's business, Elite Clothiers, occupied a North Main Street storefront in a building owned by Nigel. "I gave Ivy a break on her rent in exchange for making the costumes," he told me. "The old dear leapt at the offer."

Ivy and I are both of a certain age, but believe me it is still a long, long way from the "old dear" category. At that moment, my mind ran through its file of ten easy ways to kill a man using common household products.

When our walkie-talkies group huffed its way along Main Street two days later, I told Ivy I'd heard about the arrangement. She snorted in disgust. "A break on the rent! Hardly. He threatened to evict me unless I made the costumes and paid for the supplies."

"But then he'd be out one good tenant," I said.

"Oh no. He claimed that floozy Mimi Lure would take over the space. And then he insisted I buy all the fabric from her. She has him wrapped around her finger. He can't see past her over-exposed bosoms."

"She's quite the booby-trap," I said.

Ivy chuckled. "Definitely. But here's what galls me most—not the threat, not Mimi—Nigel said making the costumes would be a nice change from mere alterations. Mere alterations! I'm a *tailor.* Honestly, Persimmon, sometimes I'd like to make a few alterations to Nigel's face."

Lazy Days Parade Mascot Moby Duck's Magnificent Adventure

By the time the 2019 version of Lazy Days rolled around, the parade had gained notoriety. The crowd formed early for the parade. People held cameras at the ready for the unexpected. Even though the skies were clear, ninety-two-year-old Henry Jones passed out clear plastic ponchos to his fellow Homesteaders. "When you're dealing with Prince Ponzi, you can never be too prepared."

My friend Sergeant Courgette, who stood next to me on the sidewalk by the church, nodded and patted his equipment belt. I noticed a small, black, pleated object wedged into the back of his belt. "Is that…?" I asked.

"*Oui*," he said. "Umbrella. I am a police officer. Therefore, always on the lookout. Especially for the unexpected."

As usual, Nigel's Mallardmobile was sandwiched between the Lucky Duckies and the Flock of Fowl. When the Lucky Duckies emerged from the Blossom Creek Tunnel, I spotted Ivy Jinks in their jaunty yellow midst and waved at her.

"Madame Jinks has brought style to the costumes," Courgette said. "Especially the duckbill caps."

"She works magic," I said. "She once made a shopping bag for me that folds up to look exactly like a purse-sized packet of tissues. You don't know what it is until you turn it inside out."

The Mallardmobile approached the entrance to the tunnel. Taking inspiration from American Thanksgiving parades, Nigel had invested in a gigantic duck balloon that flew high above his float. Nigel gestured upward and shouted, "Let me introduce Moby Mallard, our parade mascot!"

Not unexpectedly, when a helium-filled duck as wide as a baseball diamond meets a two-lane wide space like the Blossom Creek Tunnel, problems will arise. The Mallardmobile entered the tunnel, Moby's tether cords followed. Moby bobbed above the tunnel. The cords securing the balloon to the Mallardmobile became taut and finally tore away. Freed, Moby gained altitude.

"Uh-oh," Courgette said, and pulled out his cell phone. "The mascot has escaped. I'll get someone on it."

I watched the balloon disappear over the mountains east of town. "Moby is heading for Chanterelle. I'm following. Are you coming?"

Blossom City's long-time rival, Chanterelle, held its Mushroom Magic festival at the same time as our Lazy Days. Its parade always occurred on the same day, and at the exact time, as ours. Blossom City residents who visited Chanterelle risked being called traitors. Or worse, fungus-lovers. But Moby gave me an excellent opportunity to go to Chanterelle without enraging my town: I'd simply claim I wanted to rescue the Lazy Days mascot.

Chanterelle was fifteen minutes from Blossom City as the duck flies, twenty minutes by road. However, Moby must have taken a detour or two because when Courgette and I parked near Chanterelle's main street we saw Moby cresting Oyster Hill just west of the town. His wings drooped slightly, and his head had lost its proud, upright bearing.

"Does Moby look unhappy?" I asked.

"Hmm, it appears he has sprung a leak."

We found an excellent viewing spot along the parade route. I counted three marching bands, eight floats on which children in fairy costumes danced around gayly painted toadstools, and one lone float promoting mushroom manure. Blossom City's parade had only one band. We also lacked a manure float. A final group of marchers linked arms as they lurched along, giggling, and calling "hi" to the crowd. I wondered what mushroom they were celebrating.

Moby had almost reached the parade when the Companions of the Mushroom drill team—perhaps thirty men and women, dressed in off-white uniforms, and riding kick scooters—came into view. "I suppose the chef's toques on their heads are meant to be mushroom caps," I said.

When the drill team was partway into a traditional grapevine maneuver, the parade route was suddenly cast into shadow. The spectators looked upward. "Oooooh," most said. One or two said, "Duck!"

Moby had arrived.

Courgette and I later agreed that Moby would have come to rest several miles east of Chanterelle had it not been for one dangling tether cord that managed to entangle itself around a Companion of the Mushroom's kick scooter. As the drill team wove its intricate grapevine, Moby, now tethered to a Companion and mere feet above, tagged along. The cord wound more and more tightly around the scooter, and at last Moby settled on top of the drill team, enveloping them and their scooters under his massive, partially deflated body.

After Courgette and I helped disengage Moby from the drill team, we surveyed the damage. One helium duck, now a disheartened shell of its former self. Ten bruised shins. Twelve twisted kick scooters. Thirty crushed chef's toques. One apoplectic Commander Companion of the Mushroom. "This attack is the handiwork of that malicious Mallard," she said. "Someone ought to put a death cap in his soup."

Famed Lazy Days Parade Takes Tragic Turn

Blossom City put social distancing safeguards in place for the 2020 parade, requiring all participants and spectators to wear masks, and marking circles on sidewalks where spectators could stand and be properly distant from others.

Most of us headed to South Main Street to secure prime sidewalk space near the Blossom Creek Tunnel, where we knew the unexpected could be expected to occur. I arrived early and waved at Ivy in her yellow duckling outfit. She was losing her battle to corral the giggling Lucky Duckies. A passerby commented that the tunnel lights had burned out. "If that's the extent of the unexpected, this will be a bust of a parade."

Henry Jones handed out rain gear. Sergeant Courgette tucked his collapsible umbrella into his equipment belt. Pastor Vine's congregation held signs with the words "Save Our Street, Vote Him Out" splashed across images of potholes.

This year Nigel had added a feather-covered armchair to his Mallardmobile. He sat in his throne atop the float as it travelled the route behind the cheerful and yellow costumed Lucky Duckies. He waved regally and greeted spectators. Before his float followed the Lucky Duckies into the Blossom Creek Tunnel, Nigel turned to wave and bestow a smile on his Flock of Fowl, who brought up the rear. Decked out in gray-and-teal costumes, they wore green duckbill caps and yellow masks.

Two of the smallest Lucky Duckies broke ranks and ran out from the Blossom Creek Tunnel ahead of their group. "Dark in there," one said. "But we weren't scared."

"Yeah, no way," his buddy said, just as the remainder of the Lucky Duckies spilled from the tunnel exit onto South Main Street. Several looked at the sun and cheered.

A moment later, the Mallardmobile exited the tunnel. Nigel sat on his throne and stared at his Lucky Duckies. The Flock of Fowl exited the tunnel just as the Mallardmobile's front wheel hit the pothole directly in front of the church, widely claimed to be the meanest pothole on South Main Street. Pastor Vine believed Nigel had ordered town maintenance crews to deepen that pothole, often saying, "Not only an extortionist, but spiteful."

When the wheel slammed into the hole, the Mallardmobile bounced, and Nigel slid from his throne, down the side of the float, and onto the street, where he lay, staring at the sky. The Mallardmobile continued along the parade route, its driver apparently oblivious to the fact the float had lost its passenger.

"Did Nigel hit his head?" I asked Courgette. "He might be unconscious."

By the time we reached Nigel's side, a mob of bystanders and costumed marchers surrounded him. Courgette called nine-one-one, and we pushed our way through the group. I pointed at a discoloration in the feathers of Nigel's cape. "Sergeant, what is that?"

Courgette studied Nigel and then felt for a pulse. "That is blood, madame. This was not an accident. Mr. Mallard has been murdered."

Murderer of Mayor Mallard Remains at Large

Three weeks after the parade tragedy, despite viewing countless videos and speaking with parade participants and spectators, the police had not made an arrest.

Sergeant Courgette phoned me on a Monday morning. "Persimmon, I would value your thoughts on this case. Will you join me for coffee?"

I am what sports fans would call Courgette's color commentator. Because he has lived in Blossom City for only ten years, his investigations are hindered by his lack of knowledge about the history of our town and residents. I have lived here all my life. If an investigation was a stew of ingredients, one could say I provided the seasoning necessary for Courgette's mélange to develop fully.

"I'm free this afternoon, Milton." Although I was confident that I knew the answer, I asked, "Where would you like to meet?"

"You are my guest. Your choice."

"There's a bistro I heard about. A new-age place. Vegan, dairy free, gluten-free. That kind of thing. Plus, they have outdoor seating."

"Oh, *oui*?" Courgette said. His voice had lost its upbeat tone.

"Mm-hmm. Healthy offerings. Wheatgrass and spinach smoothies to die for."

He sighed.

I went on. "And, we would have privacy. Word is they rarely have a crowd."

"I'm sure that's correct." Dejection reduced his voice to a whisper.

"Or we could go to… no, we have been there so often I'm sure you are tired of it."

His voice picked up. "*Oui?*"

"La Patisserie."

"Oh!"

"I suppose it's too much of the same old thing, Milton? Would you prefer the new-age place? Shall we expand our horizons?"

His voice crackled. "*Non!*" He took a breath. "No, Persimmon, I am prepared to deal with the familiarity of La Patisserie, if you so wish. I would hate to deprive you of the delights it offers."

I stopped playing with him then and gave him the response I knew he ached to hear. "La Patisserie, it is then. Say two o'clock?"

When I arrived at the restaurant, Sergeant Courgette had already claimed a table on the outdoor patio. A large French press of coffee and an assortment of pastries sat on the table. Two beignets, one chocolate croissant, one crème brûlée, and one slice of gâteau St. Honoré. All his favorites. It was evident which dessert he hoped I would choose.

When I slipped into the chair opposite him, he gestured at the sweets. "I was not sure what you would enjoy, so I ordered a selection."

"How thoughtful of you, Milton." He poured my coffee while I studied the pastries. When I reached toward the crème brûlée, the French press in Courgette's hand shook. I withdrew my hand.

"Hmm," I said. "Doesn't that St. Honoré look appetizing today?"

He gulped. "*Oui*, it does."

"I just can't resist," I said.

Courgette compressed his lips and stared at me. I was certain he held his breath as I reached across the table and selected a beignet.

"Ah! Excellent choice, Persimmon." He settled more comfortably in his chair and pulled the crème brûlée over.

"How is your investigation going?" I asked between sips of coffee.

Courgette replaced the now-empty brûlée dish with the St. Honoré slice. "Mr. Mallard was stabbed in the heart. It must have happened in the tunnel because you and I both saw him turn and wave to the Fowl Flock marchers before his float disappeared into the darkness."

I nodded. "That's true."

He sighed and took a bite of St. Honoré cake. "We have not found the weapon. Nor have we identified any suspects. Not even a person of interest."

"What have the witnesses told you?"

Courgette pulled his notebook from his pocket and opened it. "Mimi Lure, who was driving the float, said the Mallardmobile rocked slightly in the tunnel. She assumed she'd hit a small pothole."

And here I thought I knew everything about Blossom City and its residents. Nigel was particular about who drove his prized Mallardmobile. "Mimi was the driver?"

"Yes. Apparently, she volunteered to be a marcher, either a Ducky or a Fowl. But Ivy Jinks told her she was... well, umm... too well-endowed for the costumes."

I smiled. "Did the word 'floozy' come up?"

Courgette consulted his notebook again. "Something better. Mimi suggested Ivy could make a few alterations to a costume for her. Ivy's response was, 'Be like a duck and flock off.' Mimi was quite upset about Mr. Mallard's demise. 'Now where will I go?' she asked me."

"Did Mimi see anything?"

"Her view was limited to the road directly in front of the float. She saw the Lucky Duckies ahead of the Mallardmobile on the route until they entered the tunnel. After that she saw nothing because the lights were out. She said she slowed to a crawl because it was so dark."

"Any chance she heard something in the tunnel?"

"Only some Lucky Duckies teasing the younger ones about monsters in the tunnel and then a lot of wailing."

"And Ivy Jinks—did you interview her?"

He flicked through the notebook. "Ivy Jinks. Yes. She and Lily Plouffe were together near the back of the Fowl Flock. Neither of them saw, or heard, anything."

He took a last bite of the gâteau and raised his eyes heavenward. "Mmm. I wonder, Persimmon, if you have any ideas?"

I considered what I knew about my neighbors and their dealings with the mayor. "I'm not sure how much strength it takes to stab someone but, for a ninety-three-year-old, Henry Jones is spry. He lost money in one of Nigel's investment schemes. Have you thought about him and his fellow Homesteaders?"

Courgette shook his head. "All accounted for in their walkers and wheelchairs on the sidewalk at the parade that day. We have video to confirm it."

"Could they have hired someone?"

He chuckled. "If all sixty of them pooled their savings, perhaps they could come up with a C-team assassin."

I refilled our coffees. Courgette finished the St. Honoré and eyed the second beignet. He tilted his head and looked at me. I shook my head. "Go ahead, Milton. I've had plenty."

Courgette bit into the beignet.

"God may strike me down," I said, "but what about Pastor Vine? I don't remember seeing him among the spectators, and those potholes have driven him mad over the years."

Icing sugar exploded upward as Courgette laughed. "I remember Mallard's first parade with the ducks and the dogs and the pothole. Several eyebrows in our audit department were raised at my team's dry-cleaning expenses that year."

He wiped icing sugar from his mustache. "*Non.* Alas, the pastor has an excellent alibi. He spent the day in Chanterelle leading a retreat for the victims of last year's Moby duck debacle. Apparently, several spectators and most of the drill team are suffering from PTSD."

"I see. So, I'm guessing that also takes the Companions of the Mushroom off the suspect list."

"*Oui*. Even their fierce Commander Companion, she of the death cap threat, was at the retreat." He shook his head and blew out a breath. "We do not even have a motive for the murder. There were rumors of misguided investment advice, bad road maintenance, unfortunate parade decisions, but Mr. Mallard was not an evil man. He was more of a..."

"A booby," I said.

"Exactly."

My hand shook as I lowered my coffee cup.

Courgette said, "You've gone pale, Persimmon. Are you feeling unwell?"

"I'm fine. In your search for suspects, did you consider Ivy Jinks?"

He nodded and then shook his head. "We considered everyone who was in or around the tunnel. But as I said, she was near the back of the Fowl Flock marchers. Others would have noticed if she had run ahead to the float and stabbed Mr. Mallard."

"True. I simply don't understand why she marched with the Fowl when her costume was a yellow duckling."

"No, it was a Fowl. Gray costume, green cap. I saw it."

"But… how? I saw her before the parade. She was in yellow and organizing the Lucky Duckies."

He sighed. "Perhaps she changed her mind, decided to become a Fowl, and changed outfits before the parade began. After all, she made the costumes. I'm sure she would have extra."

"I suppose."

He went on. "In any event, it is a fact that she was amidst the Fowl and couldn't run ahead to the float without someone noticing. And no one we talked to saw anyone breaking ranks."

Courgette reached for the croissant, hesitated, and withdrew his hand. Then he shrugged and sighed. He snatched the croissant and wrapped it in a paper napkin. "For the dog," he said.

"Chocolate is bad for dogs."

"Oh, *oui?*" He grinned. "Just as well I don't have one."

I toyed with my coffee cup and thought things over. From past consultations with Sergeant Courgette, I knew we needed motive, opportunity, and means. Ivy had the means (name a seamstress who doesn't have wickedly sharp fabric shears). Motive and opportunity, however, were challenging. Still, I had an idea about both.

I leaned forward. "I have a suggestion."

Police Pinch Perpetrator of Parade Stabbing

The next day I made two telephone calls and obtained information which helped Courgette obtain a search warrant.

Then I called Ivy and invited her to my house. "I'd like you to go through my wardrobe and give me advice on what additions I should make. Are you free tomorrow morning?"

Promptly at nine the next morning, a masked-up Ivy arrived. We spent two hours pulling items from my closet and assessing them. It could have been done in less time, but I needed to drag things out while Courgette's team performed their search. Accordingly, I insisted on modelling everything for her. "You can tell me the truth, Ivy. If something doesn't fit or makes me look out-of-date, tell me. I can take it, I promise."

I had forgotten how blunt Ivy could be. "Eww, Persimmon, puce is definitely not the color for you."

And, "My heavens, what were you thinking when you bought that? With your shape, you really should avoid buying anything off the rack. And never, never anything with a peplum."

And the one that made my mind again visit the "how to off your neighborhood couturier" file: "Well yes, twenty pounds ago that might have worked."

My cell phone rang, saving Ivy from harm. She continued muttering about my bad fashion sense while I answered the call. It was Courgette.

"Madame Jinks' assistant let us in," he said. "What a migraine of a search. You said to look for *something* that was *perhaps* the size of a small satchel and *very likely* made from dark fabric. In a dressmaker's shop. Several times my officers and I wished you had been more specific. And that black was not the current rage in fashion."

"But?"

"But we persevered and found the item. We confiscated it, along with a yellow duckling costume and one dozen pairs of shears. I will be at your house shortly."

"You have no idea how happy I am to hear that," I said.

I ended the call and said to Ivy, "Turns out wardrobe culling is exhausting. Let's take a break."

We sat in my kitchen while the coffee brewed.

"It's been a while since I've seen you," I said. "Was it at the parade a few weeks ago?"

"Probably. I've been quite busy since then."

I poured two mugs of coffee. "Sugar? Cream?"

Ivy shook her head. "Fattening." She glanced at my waistline.

I sucked in my belly and slid into the chair opposite her. Giving her no chance to comment further on body shapes, I said, "I heard the strangest thing yesterday from Lily Plouffe. She said you marched with the Flock of Fowl in the parade."

Ivy nodded and blew on her coffee.

"But I remember seeing you in a duckling costume that morning. You were trying to manage the Lucky Duckies. You waved at me."

Her eyes narrowed slightly as she studied me. "That's right. But I changed my mind and decided to join the Flock of Fowl. Too many years of the same old thing, you know? I sorted out the Duckies and then changed costumes."

"Really? When did you change? Because I also spoke to Mimi Lure yesterday. Did you know she was driving the Mallardmobile? She saw you before she entered the tunnel. You were in the back row of the Duckies. Right in her line of vision. In your yellow costume."

Ivy jerked her mug and coffee splashed onto the table. "Mimi! I'm surprised Nigel would let her drive the float with her eyesight. She's mistaken."

I wiped up the coffee spill with a paper towel. "Mimi also told me Nigel had drawn up eviction papers for your shop. He planned to lease that space to her. According to her, they were an item."

"Hah! There is no way they were an item. That floozy will say anything if it helps her and hurts me. She's a liar. I changed costumes and was in the Flock of Fowl. Ask Lily, she'll confirm it."

"Actually, I did ask Lily. And she confirmed you walked beside her for part of the parade. But the first time she noticed you was when she bumped into you in the dark in the tunnel. You told her your shoelace had come undone, so you stopped to tie it. Then you tagged along beside her."

Ivy stood up. "What are you suggesting, Persimmon?"

"I think you sabotaged the tunnel lights. You marched with the Duckies until you entered the dark tunnel, then you climbed onto the float and stabbed Nigel. After that, you put a Fowl costume on over top of your yellow one, waited until the Flock came alongside and then joined them."

She laughed. "That's a lot to do in a minute or two."

"Perhaps. But I think you practiced the switch. And Mimi drove slower than usual through the tunnel because it was so dark. I think you had three or four minutes to pull it all off."

"And in those three or four minutes, where would I have found the Fowl costume to change into?"

"You hid it in the tunnel the night before the parade."

She moved along the hallway toward my front door. "I don't have to listen to this idiocy any longer. How can a person hide a duck costume in the tunnel without a pedestrian or driver noticing it? The whole idea is ridiculous."

My doorbell rang. "Don't leave yet, Ivy. I think your question is about to be answered."

I opened the door and smiled at Courgette. "Sergeant, hello. Ivy just asked me how someone could hide a duck costume in the tunnel without it being spotted."

"With this," Courgette said, and held up a large clear evidence bag containing a bulky black pouch. "My officers were not as skilled at folding the costume as you were, Madame Jinks. It is therefore rumpled now. But we have this video of its original condition."

He clicked on his phone screen so we could watch a video of an officer holding a smooth foot-square black pouch with a loop at the top. Then the officer opened a flap on the pouch and turned it inside out. The contents unfurled and became a gray and teal duck costume. When the officer shook out the costume, a green duckbill cap spilled from the middle.

"I remember the shopping bags you made several years ago," I said to Ivy. "You did the same magic with this costume. It folded into a flat pouch that you hung from a light fixture in the tunnel. In the dark it would have been invisible."

"We also found the duckling costume you wore," Courgette said. "It has deep pockets where you could hide a pair of scissors. And it has small stains on it that we believe are drops of blood. Mr. Mallard's blood."

Ivy hid her face in her hands and sank to the floor. When she finally raised her gaze to Courgette, tears streaked her cheeks. "He took everything from me. I made the costumes, I paid for all the supplies, I did everything he asked.

I rented my space and all my machines and equipment from him. He was going to evict me and give my shop and machines to Mimi. He said, 'You can keep your needles and pins. And your scissors. Maybe you can take in mending work.'"

Landslide Victory for New Mayor of Blossom City

Blossom City is slowly recovering from the trauma of Nigel's murder. We have a new mayor whose promise to rid our streets of potholes gave him a landslide victory. I'm sure Mayor-Pastor Vine can easily divide his responsibilities between the town and his church.

Many townspeople regret Nigel's death. Some, like Holly, because Nigel was the primary sponsor and organizer of the parade. To be honest, most regret his death because Ivy is now in prison and unavailable to make their clothes.

All is not lost. Holly is in discussions with the warden. She hopes the prison will permit Ivy to take in orders while she serves her time. Residents of Blossom City will undoubtedly keep her busy.

However, after Ivy's comments on my wardrobe that day at my house, I doubt I will use her services again. There are limits to how forgiving I can be.

Charlotte Morganti is a Canadian writer of crime fiction. She usually sets her stories in small towns that harbor both villains (often cunning, occasionally inept) and the sleuths who pursue them. Her short stories have been published in several anthologies, including Mystery Weekly's *Die Laughing, An Anthology of Humorous Mysteries* and Sisters in Crime-Canada West's anthology *Crime Wave*. She and her husband live in a small town on the Sunshine Coast of British Columbia.

LAST GUNFIGHT OF THE SEASON

GORDON LINZNER

Ed's death was a darn good one. His best to date. His grimace was realistic, the spin timed perfectly. You couldn't see his hands reach out to soften the impact, a common mistake. He landed perfectly in front of the bank building across from the Last Chance Saloon, face down, even raising a tiny puff of dirt.

I figured he'd been practicing.

I'm a bit of an expert on dying. It was how I made my living for six years, before I got promoted to sheriff of Frontier City. Now the most I'm allowed is to get shot in the arm, which doesn't leave much room for improvisation. As the hero, I'm supposed to bear pain stoically. Still, the pay is better, and I can interact more with the park visitors. Bad guys don't have that option.

Only when the pool of red spread further from his body than our stage blood capsules could allow did I realize why Ed's performance seemed so convincing.

I went off-script, firing blanks into the air to let the other actors know something was wrong. Charlie had already risen from the dead, by the stable, to hurry toward Ed.

"Don't touch him!" I warned. "Phil, Abe, keep the crowd back." Not that there was much of a crowd. Frontier City would close today until the spring. We had maybe a dozen paying families in the entire park. Our gunfight nearly outnumbered the observers.

I sent Mel to the barber shop to fetch the park's medic. This late in the season, with summer interns dismissed, we all did double or triple duty. Doc Jefferson wore the undertaker's suit, and hated every minute of it, though his sour expression fit the role. He rushed to bend over Ed's still form. A minute later, he told us what we already knew.

"He's dead, George." Then Doc Jefferson added something unexpected. "He's been shot in the back."

* * * *

The Ansac County sheriff arrived within fifteen minutes of our call. I was in charge by default, herding almost everybody into the saloon. Three of the visiting families refused to stay with a killer on the loose. I couldn't argue their point. I took names, home addresses, and the motels at which they were staying, and assured them they'd only be contacted if absolutely necessary. Knowing Sheriff Stone, they'd likely be dragged back in less than an hour.

Also present was Ed's wife Mae. She'd stopped by as usual to pick up her husband after the day's last gunfight. She waited stoically, taking the news of her husband's death fairly well.

Disturbingly well.

"I'm not going to get hysterical, George." She acted more annoyed at my attempt to read her emotionless face. "Ed and I haven't gotten along these past few months. I'm sorry he's dead, but I won't pretend to grieve."

"Fair enough, Mae." Mae Rivers was too proud to go to pieces in public. She covered her mouth with one hand, looking ready to chew a fingernail. Then she made a distasteful face and let it drop.

"Still haven't broken the habit?" I asked.

"Working on it." She took a small glass container from her purse and brushed clear liquid on her nails. "This stuff tastes so horrible, it just might work. Wears off too fast, though. I have to keep replacing it."

That's when Sheriff Stone called me into Bristol's office.

Johnny Bristol, manager and half-owner of Frontier City, was not smiling. I couldn't remember seeing my portly employer without his trademark idiotic grin. He even smiled when he fired people.

"The sheriff wants to ask you some questions, George. Just answer them, all right?"

As if I had other options.

I told Stone what I'd seen, in detail, and handed him my list of park visitors. He glanced at the paper, folded it into his notepad, and turned back to Bristol. "Who checks the guns are loaded with blanks?"

Bristol shrugged. "George handles the routine matters. I'm here for PR and emergencies. Most of my time is spent bookkeeping."

"In the summer months," I added, "we have a regular prop man. This late in the season we double up on responsibilities. Each of us loads his own gun from the blanks in the locker room behind the general store. I already collected the guns from today's show and brought them to Mr. Bristol."

Stone grunted. "I saw. One of my deputies is taking them to the county lab. They'd obviously all been fired. Any of you could have substituted a real bullet for a blank."

The thought had also occurred to me, but I resented his tone. "Or had it replaced later. Or mixed in with the blanks by accident."

Stone shook his head. "That's weak, George, and you know it. Substituting real bullets in someone else's gun wouldn't guarantee Ed, or anyone, would be hit, let alone killed. You don't seriously aim at any of your opponents, do you?"

"Just the general direction. Safety protocols."

"Uh huh. Ever tried shooting a loaded gun one-handed?"

"Couple times. Didn't hit anything."

"Takes lots of practice, or you have to get pretty close. Ed Rivers was shot in the back, dead center. Can't tell me that was an accident. Did you notice if anyone fired two-handed?"

"No. Undercuts the drama."

Stone grunted again. "All right. You can go."

"No, sir." I knew always to be polite when contradicting a supervisor, a customer, or the law.

"Beg pardon?"

"I want to stay. You're accusing one of Frontier City's staff of murder, somebody I've worked with. I need to see your suspects get a fair shake."

Bristol leaned forward. "George, this is not the time to take that tin star seriously. You're not the real law."

I unclipped my sheriff's badge and tossed it onto Bristol's desk. "Never said I was. But unless you've got a good reason for kicking me out, sheriff, like I'm your prime suspect, I want to stay. Otherwise, I won't believe it's possible."

Stone glanced at me, then at the cheap, badly-dented tin badge. He chuckled, surprising both Bristol and myself. I guess my act did look ludicrously dramatic, like a scene from a second-rate western.

"All right, George," the sheriff said. "You can stay, but only if you keep quiet. Your boss and I might know something about your fellow employees you don't."

As a courtesy, Stone first interviewed the families who'd volunteered to stay. Bristol handed the children Indian headdresses, Frontier City all-day suckers, and Colt .45 water pistols. The latter seemed a particularly unfortunate choice, but no one commented, least of all the parents. They were just grateful the questioning was brief.

Stone just as quickly dismissed the four employees—our gift shop hostess, stable boy, and two short-order cooks at the snack bar—who had been elsewhere at the time, and only spoke with Doc Jefferson long enough to ensure there would be no discrepancy with the medical examiner's preliminary report.

"So," the sheriff asked each actor separately, "you didn't look at Charlie, because you assumed he was playing dead?"

"That's right," confirmed Abe. "Can I escort Mae to her car now? She's anxious to get home."

"Go. I already spoke to her."

"I was watching George," explained Mel. "He was supposed to cut me down next. Sorry, George, didn't mean it that way."

"Didn't pay attention." Phil bit his lower lip.

"Tell the sheriff what you saw last week, Phil," Bristol urged. Phil looked away uncomfortably.

"Your boss already told me, Phil," Stone assured him. "I just need your confirmation."

Phil sighed. "I'm sorry I said anything. It's none of my business. Just the initial shock..."

Bristol stood up to pat Phil's shoulder. "You did the right thing. I've got to know about such goings-on."

"Well, last Thursday I ran late. You had that doctor's appointment, George, and I'd had to wrangle a lost child. I was changing to my civvies when I heard voices from the shower room. I moseyed over—and saw Ed and Charlie. They were...I don't want to say it. They were too busy to notice me, though."

Stone turned to me. "Did you know about Ed and Charlie, George? No, I see by your face you didn't."

"Mae thought there might be another woman. It never occurred to me..."

Bristol interrupted. "I called both men into my office, separately. I said I knew what was going on—didn't mention your name, Phil—and ordered them to stop, at least on the premises, or I'd fire them both. Ed refused to say anything. Charlie got defensive and apologetic."

"Charlie can be high-strung," I commented.

Stone nodded. "You can go for now, Phil. Tell Charlie Sommers to come in."

Stone's questioning turned brutally direct.

"Yeah, I'm gay," Charlie responded. "I'm not ashamed of it, the way Ed was. If anyone asked me direct, I'd have told them. But I wasn't going to advertise. I've lost more than one job because of unsympathetic bosses like you, Bristol!"

"I don't care about your personal problems," Bristol countered. "Frontier City has a family-friendly image to maintain."

"Only people like you think it's a problem. I'm fine with my sex life!"

Stone's voice echoed in the small office. "Time out! We're getting off track. The point is, Charlie, your affair with Ed gives you a motive for killing him."

"What?" Charlie collapsed in his chair.

"Do you deny being upset with Ed after Bristol's talk?"

"Of course not. I thought Ed was throwing me to the wolves to keep his job. I didn't mind being exposed; it was the hurt of the betrayal."

"Did you threaten to kill him?"

"Not seriously."

"But you did threaten?"

"I was upset. I said I'd like to kill him. Didn't mean it. George! How often have I said I wanted Bristol dead?"

I started to speak. Stone waved me silent. "Bristol isn't the murder victim. Ed Rivers is."

"I know." Charlie sank into his chair. "I saw him die."

"You were nearest to him?"

"I guess so. I know I reached him first."

"George told us. Weren't you also the only gunfighter directly *behind* Ed?"

"Of course! I went down first. But we started out side by side, advancing on George and Abe. That's how the show ran."

"Convenient for you. And no one paid attention to you after you fell."

"Why would they? I was out of the action."

"So it wouldn't have been difficult for you to fire a shot at Ed, maybe using your body to conceal the weapon in case someone did look your way?"

"I didn't!"

Stone pulled a plastic bag from the satchel sitting on Bristol's desk. He dangled it in front of Charlie. "Recognize the contents?"

"A western glove. Brown leather."

"You have one like it?"

"Don't bait me, sheriff. If C S is initialed on the inside, you already know it belongs to me."

Stone pointed to the black mark near the thumb. "That's a fresh powder burn, Charlie, a big one. No blank cartridge is responsible for that."

"Except I wore my tan gloves today. Couldn't find my dark brown ones. Do you have the mate, as well?"

Stone turned at me. "George, is that true?"

I glanced at Charlie, shrugged helplessly. "I'd like to help, Charlie, but I didn't pay attention to what you were wearing. Even if I had, those colors are pretty close."

Charlie snorted in disgust.

"Let's finish this at the station, Charlie. We've got motive, means, opportunity and"—Stone waggled the bag with the glove—"evidence. I'm guessing we'll have more once we check the bullet in Ed's spine against your gun."

After telling me to instruct the others to stop by the sheriff's office to sign statements, Stone and a deputy led Charlie Sommers out the front door of the Last Chance Saloon.

* * * *

I found Abe, the last Frontier City employee to whom I needed to deliver Stone's injunction, in the locker room behind the general store.

"I was worried about Mae," he explained. "She was too chill. I was afraid she'd do something crazy on the road, so I drove her home and took a cab back to get my own car. I didn't know everyone had left."

"Stone still wants statements. But he thinks he's got Charlie cold."

"Hard to believe. That Charlie would kill Ed, I mean. That other stuff, I had suspicions."

"I hadn't noticed. Guess I'll never be a real lawman."

"Ever changed clothes in the same room with him?"

I confessed I hadn't; Charlie joined us after my promotion. My private locker was in the back of the sheriff's office.

Abe finished changing into street clothes and neatly folded his western outfit for the winter. A piece of bright yellow cardboard stuck out of a back pocket. With a frown, he pulled it out and handed it to me.

"Doesn't matter now," he said, "but who wired the cardboard signs to the bumpers this morning?"

"Mel, I think."

"Well, someone should remind him how much Mae hates these things. Lucky she didn't notice. I took it off her car as I left her place. Have a good night!"

"You too." I perched on a short wooden bench alongside the lockers, studying the crumpled cardboard. I'd seen thousands of these: the legend "Visit Frontier City off route 27" in gaudy yellow and orange on a black background. This one bothered me, though I didn't know why. I took it to my sheriff's office to compare it with the ones in my desk.

Half an hour was wasted, comparing that bumper card to a fresh one. The former was badly tattered. Gray cardboard lines showed beneath the printing where Abe had folded it. I held it up to the light, held both versions up to a mirror. Except for the wear, I saw not a shred of difference between them.

Once I admitted that to myself, the answer was clear.

Cursing my stupidity, I leapt from my chair and raced out the door.

Frontier City was deathly quiet, myself presumably the sole inhabitant. The western mock-up buildings looked cheerlessly unreal in the September twilight. A chill hint of impending frost underscored the desolate mood.

I felt this sensation at the end of every season, though, so paid no attention to the eerie shadows now.

I circled behind the general store, used my passkey to open the locker room's back door. Eschewing overhead lights, I used my flashlight to locate Charlie's locker.

The locker door swung partially open. I was certain it had been closed when I spoke to Abe. I pulled it fully open and ran my flashlight beam over the contents.

A pair of tan gloves lay neatly folded on a shelf. Tucked into the back corner, as if trying to hide, sat a single brown glove, definitely darker. I tucked the flashlight under my arm, picked up the brown glove, turned it inside out. Gingerly, I touched my tongue to the fingertips.

A sharp bitter taste rewarded me.

My idea proved, I considered the implications of the open locker. My brain finally started working.

"Come on out, Mae," I called. "It's over."

Part of an eye peeked out from the entrance to the shower room. For the first time I could recall, Mae's voice quavered. "How did you know I was here?"

"There aren't enough nails in Charlie's coffin to satisfy you, Mae? What other evidence are you trying to plant?"

She shifted slightly. I could make out a whole eye now, reflecting my flashlight's beam. I didn't want to scare her off; I wanted to make it easy for her to confess.

"You're bluffing," she insisted. "You don't know anything. I'm here to collect my husband's things. Accidentally opened the wrong locker. That's all."

"Not good enough, Mae. Abe showed me the placard he took off your car. Mel does his parking lot rounds before the gunfight, not after. You must have arrived at least a half hour earlier than you claimed. I think you entered the park the back way—not hard to do, given our lack of staff—and hid in one of the buildings. The bank, most likely, where Ed fell. You killed him, Mae."

"That's a nice fantasy tale."

"You found out about Ed and Charlie. Another woman, maybe, you could accept, but Ed cheating on you with a man was too much for your pride. You knew it was bound to come out; maybe Ed even threatened to make it public, pressure you into a divorce."

"You can't prove anything except that I got here early. I could've been sitting in my car that whole time."

"No. You'd have seen Mel, told him where to put his bumper sticker. I think you broke in here, used Charlie's spare costume for camouflage. I know you wore his gloves. There are traces of your anti-chewing nail polish inside this one. The sheriff's lab will find them in the other as well."

"Not if he doesn't know what to look for!"

At the glint of gun-metal, I flashed my light in her face. Blinded, her shot went wild, ricocheting off a locker behind me.

She next aimed for the flashlight. I dropped it and rolled forwards, trying to fox her into thinking she'd hit me while at the same time getting close enough to disarm her.

My plan failed. The locker area was too narrow for the fancy falls I employed in the wide streets of Frontier City. I landed not on soft packed dirt but hard, unyielding shower tiles. To compound matters, Mae kicked at my stomach as I flew past. I would never be able to avoid her next shot.

Light suddenly flooded both shower and locker room.

Sheriff Stone stood in the entryway, a police special in his hand. In both hands. He winked at me.

"Drop the gun, Mae," he ordered.

She blinked, cursed, and placed it on the floor. I managed to catch my breath, retrieve her weapon, and bring it to Stone, staying clear of his line of fire. Then I sank onto the bench.

"Is this the same gun you used to kill your husband, Mae?"

"That's not what's happening here, Sheriff," she pleaded. "I came here to collect some of Ed's personal things. George had just taken this gun out of Charlie's locker. I think those two have got some side action going on. George is trying to cover up for his friend."

"Oh, shut up," I snapped at her, frustrated.

"No, let her talk," Stone chided. "She's saying some mighty interesting things."

"Sheriff, you don't really believe..."

"Quiet, George. I want to hear her explain that conversation I overheard before the shooting started."

Mae went silent.

Stone continued. "You see, Mae, ballistics couldn't match the bullet in Ed to Charlie's gun, so I came back to look for another weapon. You claim George here took this gun out of Charlie's locker. Problem is, my men went through that locker with a fine-tooth comb after the arrest. Not to mention going through all the lockers on our arrival. And how a frail little girl like you could wrestle a gun away from a big old hunk like George is beyond me."

"The nail polish," I wheezed. My gut started feeling better. "Check her purse. She's got some stuff that should match the inside of Charlie's glove."

"So I heard." Stone raised a hand. Two deputies appeared behind him. "Take Mrs. Rivers to the car, boys. I'll join you in a minute."

When they'd gone, Sheriff Stone settled onto the bench next to me. "How're you feeling?"

"Shaky," I admitted. "Embarrassed at being caught with my pants down. Otherwise, okay."

"Still turning in your badge?"

I smiled feebly. "What? After devoting my life to cleaning up the streets of Frontier City?"

"That's the spirit," Stone said, punching my shoulder. "Us law folk gotta stick together."

Gordon Linzner is founder and former editor of *Space and Time Magazine*, and author of three published novels and scores of short stories in *F&SF*, *Twilight Zone*, *Sherlock Holmes Mystery Magazine*, and numerous other magazines and anthologies. He is a member of the Horror Writers Association and a lifetime member of the Science Fiction & Fantasy Writers Association.

IT CAME UPON A MIDNIGHT ICE STORM

N.M. CEDEÑO

I was Betty-Crockered-out, wishing I hadn't volunteered to host Christmas Eve dinner, when I answered the door and found a pair Dallas Police officers on the porch instead of my tardy guests. Drying my hands on my holly-patterned apron, I asked, "Can I help you?"

"Someone here called nine-one-one to report a theft," the taller of two officers said.

"You must have the wrong address."

"Is this 14527 Rosebush Lane?" he asked.

Joe, my husband, emerged from the hall behind me and said, "You got here faster than I expected. Come in out of the weather. You must be cold."

I smiled to myself at the sound of concern in his voice. Joe, an accountant and avid gardener, genuinely cared for other people, which was one of the traits that led to me marrying him a mere six months earlier. This would be our first Christmas as husband and wife.

Standing aside, I allowed the policemen entry. As I attempted to close the storm door, an icy blast ripped it open. The winter storm predicted for tomorrow was arriving prematurely. I yanked the storm door shut and muttered a desperate plea that the roads didn't ice. No one in the Dallas-Fort Worth Metroplex can drive on ice. After closing the inner door I asked, "What the heck is going on?"

"I'm sorry, Eleanor," Joe said, running an agitated hand through his thinning, dark hair. "I was going to tell you, but Sam's girlfriend Gillian is hyperventilating. We're trying to calm her down."

Mystified, I said, "She's hyperventilating? What does this have to do with a theft? Did someone break in while I was cooking? I couldn't have missed that!"

"No one broke in! Gillian lost her bracelet, freaked out, and called nine-one-one." Joe turned to the officers who were listening attentively. "Everyone is searching the game room for the missing bracelet, except Gillian, who collapsed on the floor. Follow me."

* * * *

I glanced around the game room as I entered, reading it as I read my classrooms of students at the high school and wincing as I sensed how the atmosphere had altered from festive to strained. In the middle of the room knelt Sam, my husband's twenty-five-year-old brother, reassuring his girlfriend, Gillian, who was prostrate on the floor. Gillian was breathing in abrupt staccato gasps and blubbering incoherently. Sam, attired in a gaudy holiday sweater over jeans, clutched her hand anxiously. He and Gillian had arrived at my house in Dallas that morning after driving over from Fort Worth, where Sam worked as an engineer and Gillian as a dietitian.

Four people, including my husband Joe, had been interrupted while playing penny ante poker. Their game lay abandoned on the card table. My cousin Helene, an elegant, blond lawyer with chic clothing, was crawling under the card table searching the floor. Earlier, she had been trouncing Joe, Joe's sister Becky, and Becky's boyfriend, Ernie, at Texas hold 'em.

Across the room by the television, twenty-one-year-old, red-haired Becky was removing cushions from the couch and vigorously shaking them. With fierce blue eyes and a passionate nature, Becky was majoring in biology at the University of Texas at Dallas. Ernie, a business graduate student with an easy smile and unflappable demeanor that matched well with his slow, Louisiana accent, replaced the cushions for her as she finished with them.

Nearby in a recliner lounged Joe's twenty-three-year-old youngest brother, Luke, an athlete and jokester immobilized by recent surgery on his left ankle, which he'd injured playing professional soccer. His bandaged, booted foot was elevated, resting on a pillow. The movie Luke had been watching was paused while he suggested places to search.

Crouching near Gillian, the taller police officer introduced himself as Cornell and his shorter, Hispanic partner as Santos. "Do you need medical attention?" Officer Cornell asked.

Gillian fought to control her breathing. "I'm fine, but my bracelet is gone! You have to find it!"

I choked on a sarcastic comment and shot Joe an annoyed look. If my bracelet vanished, I wouldn't call the police, I'd look for it! I had pegged Gillian as a spoiled drama queen when Sam introduced her to me upon their arrival. Somehow, Sam always fell for self-absorbed beauties. *Ugh!*

Joe gave me a sympathetic grin and began searching the room for the bracelet.

"Focus on breathing, ma'am. What's your name?" Cornell asked Gillian.

"Gillian Planter," she managed to say between breaths.

"Could you describe the missing jewelry?" he asked.

"It's a gold bracelet with rubies and emeralds in the shape of four poinsettias." Gillian's voice cracked. She struggled to sit up. "It's my favorite Christmas bracelet."

"Did it come off in your pocket or snag on your clothes?" Sam asked, his eyes inspecting Gillian's red cashmere sweater and well-defined curves.

Gillian patted her tight sweater like a B-movie starlet. Then, she inverted the pockets on her gray wool slacks. "It's not here," she whined.

Officer Cornell asked Gillian the approximate value of the bracelet.

Gushing fresh tears, she said, "My dad's going to kill me. It cost fifty thousand. It's not insured! I couldn't afford the premium, so the policy lapsed."

A stunned silence ensued.

Cornell, recovering speech, asked, "Has the bracelet ever fallen off?"

"No! It doesn't fall off!" A look of fear flashed across Gillian's face. "Someone *must* have taken it!" She sobbed and began to hyperventilate again.

Luke rolled his eyes. Becky, outraged, smothered a cry of annoyance as Sam hovered anxiously next to Gillian.

Great, she accused us of stealing instead of taking responsibility for losing her bracelet. Are you kidding me?

Officer Cornell continued his inquiry. "Where did you last have the bracelet?"

Gillian sniffled raggedly. "On the couch. I showed it to Luke."

Right then, Ernie and Joe lifted the couch. Becky searched the floor beneath it but found nothing.

"Did you leave the couch?" Cornell asked.

"I went to the kitchen, to ask Eleanor if I could help. She didn't need assistance, so I went to the living room to talk to my boyfriend, Sam, by the Christmas tree. He was putting some gifts he'd wrapped under the tree." She squeezed Sam's hand. "We needed to talk about going to see my family tomorrow."

Officer Santos said to me, "With your permission, ma'am, we can help you search. I suggest half the group search the kitchen and the rest search the living room."

I glanced at Joe, who nodded, and I said, "Yes. Let's find this bracelet."

Joe and my cousin Helene followed Santos to the living room. Sam helped the whimpering Gillian to her feet, and they went to the living room, too. Becky, her boyfriend Ernie, and I followed Officer Cornell into the kitchen. Luke, grabbing his crutches, followed.

We searched the kitchen in five minutes. A white-tiled kitchen with white cabinets and white marble countertops, to my regret, reveals more than it conceals. However, delicious aromas emanated from the food. Being recently married, this was my first Christmas Eve as hostess. I'd been cooking all day, making puff pastry appetizers and hoping I got the timing right on the food. I checked the temperature on the beef and left it roasting before walking to the living room, which was decorated heavily for Christmas.

The living room is a rectangle at the front of the house with a fireplace on one wall. Joe and the officers were searching the chocolate-colored couch and wingback chairs, which were arrayed before the hearth. Helene and Becky were shifting figurines in the Nativity display arranged on a nearby hutch. The Baby Jesus figurine was wrapped in red cloth from head to toe. My husband insisted that the Child stay covered until Christmas Day since he isn't supposed to be born yet. This was Joe's family tradition that we decided to continue to the delight of Joe's siblings.

The Christmas tree was centered before a double window overlooking the front yard. Beneath the twinkling, decorated tree, Ernie and Sam were on their knees. They shifted wrapped gifts and lifted the tree skirt. Gillian, who'd recovered her breath, rifled the Christmas tree, searching among the ornaments and lights.

Outside the window, the storm worsened. Wind howled and freezing rain began coating everything.

We ransacked the living room in vain. I even searched the stockings hung on the mantle. Finally, Luke abandoned the search and sat on the couch, elevating his foot. Everyone else half-heartedly rechecked every nook and cranny.

Luke called out from the couch, "I know who did it."

We all looked at him.

"The Grinch," he said, grinning.

I resisted the urge to throw a pillow at him.

"Or Gremlins?" he asked in a teasing tone.

Everyone groaned.

"It's a lost bracelet, not a lost World Cup championship," Luke said. "We'll find it. Lighten up."

My cell phone rang and I answered. My missing guests were calling to apologize for not coming. My aunt and uncle, Helene's parents, refused to drive in an ice storm. Terminating the call, I noticed the time. *Oh, no, the roast beef!* As I rushed toward the kitchen, Officer Santos stopped me and asked me where I was going.

"To check the roast," I said, smothering an annoyed retort. *Why was he treating losing a bracelet like a jewel heist?*

After swiftly glancing at his partner, Santos joined me in the kitchen. The thermometer told me the roast was well-done. I'd been aiming for medium-rare. I sighed and removed it from the oven, then checked the other dishes. The broccoli I set to steam before the police arrived was soggy. *Ffff ... fiddlesticks!*

Santos and I reentered the living room as Gillian insisted that someone must have taken the bracelet off her wrist.

Officer Cornell cast a doubtful eye at her. "How could someone take it without you noticing?"

Gillian stood in the middle of the room and tossed her head with exasperation. "A pickpocket stole it in London without me knowing. I only got it back because the police raided a pawn shop the next day."

Becky, with angry sparks glittering in her blue eyes, demanded, "Do we look like pickpockets to you?"

Gillian eyed each of us, biting her pouty lower lip. To my dismay, she was considering the question.

Officers Santos and Cornell were conferring near the entryway. Before Gillian could respond, Santos said, "I need everyone's identification."

I glared at Gillian. "You must have gone somewhere else in the house. The bracelet *must* have fallen off somewhere."

"I went to the bathroom, and Sam showed me the house, but I had my bracelet after that, because I showed it to Luke." Gillian pointed to Luke.

"That's true," Luke said from the couch, his crutches discarded on the floor. "Gillian showed me the bracelet as my movie was starting. She must have lost it in the hour between then and when she realized it was gone."

"You didn't see it fall off and decide it would be funny to hide it?" I asked Luke, knowing he enjoyed pranks.

"Nope," Luke said. "I still think it was the Grinch."

"Or Gremlins. Right," I said with a touch of sarcasm. My food was overcooked, and I was in no mood for his sense of humor.

Out of the corner of my eye, I saw Cornell taking notes.

Besides Luke, Helene and I admitted noticing the bracelet. Sam saw the bracelet when he drove Gillian to our house. I was surprised Becky didn't notice it, too. *Becky loves gemstones.*

I said to Gillian, "I served the appetizers at six fifteen. You followed me into the kitchen, then joined Sam by the Christmas tree in the living room. You discovered your bracelet was missing, returned to the game room, panicked, and called the police. Is that right?"

"Yes." Gillian's lip quivered.

"What did you do between showing the bracelet to Luke and coming into the kitchen?" I asked.

"I didn't feel like watching some old movie with Luke. So, I watched the card game for a little while."

"Old movie?" Luke protested, offended. "*Die Hard* is a Christmas classic!"

"Can we continue this over dinner?" Joe said, interrupting. "It's after seven, and I'm hungry."

"Would you join us?" I asked the officers. "I made plenty of food: rolls, mashed potatoes, roast beef, gravy, a tossed salad, steamed broccoli, and we have chocolate cake for dessert."

Officer Santos was finished getting everyone's names and addresses. He glanced at Cornell.

"Thank you, ma'am, but we can't," Cornell said. "We've been called to assist with traffic. Lots of accidents in this weather. Also, the Dallas County Office of Emergency Management has asked that all non-essential personnel stay off the roads. Everyone should remain here tonight."

Joe and Luke groaned simultaneously as both Gillian and Becky gasped. I stifled a sigh.

"No midnight mass, Eleanor," Helene said with disappointment. I patted her shoulder.

The two policemen walked toward the front door, and Joe and I hurried to escort them out. At the door, Cornell said, "A detective will be here in the morning to ask more questions."

"Thank you," Joe said politely, then wished them a good night.

After the officers left, Joe and I returned to the dining room where everyone stood waiting. Finally, we could eat, but what kind of dinner conversation could we have if Gillian thought we were all jewel thieves? I preferred the free-spirited banter that normally flowed at family gatherings, but I figured that was unlikely.

* * * *

We sat around the dining table, which I'd set with my grandmother's china. After the prayer, Becky, like a dog on the defensive, growled at Gillian, "You never answered my question. Which of us do you think is a pickpocket?"

Gillian regarded her with a wary expression. "It could be any one of you. You can't tell who may be a criminal by appearances."

Sam, next to Gillian, turned red with embarrassment and looked as if he wanted to disappear. "Gillian, please. My family didn't take your bracelet." He whispered the word "sorry" to his sister Becky, whose mouth was pressed into a flat line.

I cringed as conversation ceased. I hate awkward dinners. The only way forward was to continue asking questions, to demonstrate that no one took the bracelet. "Gillian, did Joe, Helene, Becky, or Ernie have a chance to take your bracelet while you were watching them play poker?"

"Wait a minute," Becky said, but stopped when her boyfriend Ernie, always a calming influence on her, squeezed her arm.

"I didn't get that close to the table. I circled it," Gillian said.

"So, none of them could have taken your bracelet. Right?" I said.

With her eyes pinched almost shut, Gillian said, "They could have helped the thief hide it."

Gillian's answer didn't faze me, but Becky spluttered in protest. Ernie placed a soothing hand over her arm again.

I gave Ernie a grateful smile. If Becky exploded at Gillian, I wouldn't be able to sort this mess out. Thank goodness Ernie could keep a cool head and help restrain Becky's temper. "OK," I said. "Barring a conspiracy, none of the card players could have stolen the bracelet. And Luke isn't mobile enough to have taken it and hidden it. That leaves me and Sam." People were still chewing the slightly tough roast. Maybe I could sort this out by the time we finished dessert.

"How about you, Sam?" I asked, annoyed that he'd inflicted Gillian on us, but trying to eliminate the note of censure from my voice. This wasn't the first time his choice of dates made for an interesting family get-together.

Sam's face colored brighter than his tacky sweater. "We talked by the Christmas tree. I didn't have time to wrap the gifts before we left, so I was doing that while the others played poker. When I finished, I went to put everything under the tree. Gillian met me there. I suppose a professional pickpocket could have taken the bracelet off her," he said, offering Gillian a placating half-smile, "but I didn't, and y'all didn't either. It fell off."

His sister Becky chimed in. "I agree, Sam. None of us took it. Right, Ernie?"

"Yes," Ernie said in his always unruffled manner and slow Louisiana accent. "She lost it."

I said, "I saw Gillian when I served appetizers and drinks, and when she came to the kitchen, but I didn't take her bracelet either. If no one took it, it must have fallen off. It will be found." Pleased with myself and my reasoning, I grinned at my husband, who gave me a supportive thumb's up, and I turned my attention back to my food.

As everyone finished eating, I asked, "Anyone want chocolate cake? Helene made it." I tried to sound cheerful and inject some good spirits back into the meal. Our first Christmas may not have been going as planned, but it was still salvageable.

Becky stared at Helene with both eyebrows raised, knowing Helene, as a newly minted lawyer, didn't have the time or interest to bake. "Since when do you bake?"

Helene chuckled at Becky's surprise. "I cheated with a cake mix recipe. And, I decorated it with a simple shake of red sugar-crystal sprinkles. I'll help serve." She rose and helped me distribute wedges of chocolate cake on dessert plates.

As soon as the chocolate hit my palate I started to relax. However, my unstressed state was fleeting.

Luke said, "What's this?" He plucked a gigantic, red sugar crystal from his cake. "Is that a ruby?" He cleaned frosting from the marquis-cut stone with his napkin and gave it to Gillian.

"This is mine." Gillian narrowed her eyes. "See! Someone must have dropped the stone while stealing my bracelet." She stared fiercely at Helene. "You decorated the cake."

Helene's perfect nose flared and red spots lit her cheeks. "If I stole a bracelet, I wouldn't serve the jewels to people to eat! Maybe you caught your bracelet on something in the kitchen, and a jewel fell onto the cake when the bracelet came off."

Becky giggled nervously and studied her cake. "What if there are more rubies?"

We scrutinized the sugar crystals on our cake slices, looking for more stones, before cautiously eating our cake. Then, Helene, Joe, and I eyeballed every red crystal on the unserved portion of cake, inspected the leftover food, and cleared the table. No more jewels appeared.

After dinner I dragged Luke aside as he hobbled by me and gave him my best teacher's glare. "If you did this to be funny, so help me—"

"No, Eleanor! This definitely isn't funny."

Studying his eyes, I detected a glint of commiseration, but couldn't decide if he was telling the truth. He was several years older and more experienced than the student pranksters I was used to handling. As we joined the others in the living room, my brain was whirling with questions and confusion.

Gillian glowered at us. "One of you probably has my bracelet in your pocket."

My husband Joe calmly turned out his pockets. "Would you like to search me?"

I followed his lead, as did everyone else. We looked ridiculous with our pockets hanging out.

Gillian lifted her chin haughtily and crossed her arms under the ample cleavage displayed by the V neck of her red sweater. "You could have hidden it anywhere."

Joe, taking in Gillian's anger and my distress, asked, "Should we search the house again?"

I pulled myself together, tired of my party being hijacked, and made my decision. "No more searching right now. We can watch a movie, or play card games, board games, or video games."

Groups formed and broke away. Helene and I washed dishes. Becky played Scrabble with Joe in the living room. Ernie, Sam, and Luke chose video games in the game room so that Luke could elevate his foot on the recliner. Gillian joined the men at the video games, criticizing their play rather than participating.

While the others were distracted, Helene and I searched the kitchen again. I was determined to find that missing bracelet. Helene opened and searched cabinets while I checked inside the drawers. Still, we found nothing.

I leaned against the counter, slouching dejectedly. "If that ruby was on the cake, the bracelet was in this kitchen at some point."

"Agreed." Helene rose from kneeling in front of a cabinet she had emptied and refilled.

I noticed that Helene left everything more organized than she found it. She even sorted my plasticware. I almost wished she would search my clothes closet.

Standing with her hands on her hips, Helene searched the room with her eyes. "I don't know what to think, Eleanor. I was sure the bracelet fell off, and we'd find it eventually. Then that ruby turned up on the cake. I've replayed the evening in my mind. The only one who left the room for an extended period was Sam when he was supposed to be wrapping gifts."

I rejected the thought that my husband's brother could have stolen his girlfriend's bracelet. "No! He wouldn't." Then, I paused, remembering a phone call a few days earlier. "Oh, I hate this. Sam might be in debt. We got a call from a debt collector looking for him. Joe called Sam and argued with him about it."

Helene put one hand on her cheek. "Damn. Do you want me to search the guest room where he was wrapping gifts?"

Miserably, I nodded. "Yes. I'll finish in here. Be discreet, okay?"

Helene slipped quietly out of the kitchen to search the guest room.

An hour later, the kitchen was clean and thoroughly searched, and Helene returned from her quest with nothing to report. The men had finished playing video games, and Gillian sat observing the last of the Scrabble game. Becky was directing perturbed glances at Gillian between plays.

As the word game ended, I called out, "Come gather by the Christmas tree, y'all. We have gifts to exchange."

Everyone seemed subdued except Luke, who paused next to the tree and swung himself on his crutches. "I'm 'Rockin' around the Christmas Tree,'" he joked, breaking the tension.

Everyone laughed except Gillian.

Joe handed out the gifts. Soon, the sound of tearing paper mingled with the noise from the ice storm outside. Everyone paused when Becky shrieked and jumped up to kiss Ernie, thanking him for sapphire earrings. Joe and I exchanged a look of surprise. Ernie was paying for graduate school and was unemployed until recently. Only last week, Becky confided that she didn't expect anything from him because of his tight finances.

Once the discarded wrapping paper was collected, I checked the time. It was a quarter to ten. *Time to discuss sleeping arrangements.*

"Luke," I said, "you should take the master bedroom tonight. That mattress will be best for your bad leg. Joe and I will use an air mattress in here by the Christmas tree."

Luke met my eyes, "Thanks for having room at your inn, Eleanor."

"You're welcome." I gave him a smile, feeling suddenly grateful for his sense of humor.

"Eleanor, can I have the bed in the guest room?" Gillian asked. She eyed Sam darkly before giving him a cold shoulder, "I want to be alone."

"Yes, that's fine." Under the circumstances, she was better off isolated than sharing space with others.

Joe announced, "We're happy to have everyone stay the night, though we may be a little crowded. We also have two camping mattresses, a recliner, and a fold-out sofa bed in the game room." He eyed his siblings, Becky and Sam. "You can decide who sleeps where. Draw straws, flip a coin."

While Joe opened the sofa-bed, Helene and I gathered pillows, linens, camping mattresses, and sleeping bags, and distributed them. When I returned to the living room, Joe and Sam had moved the wingback chairs and were inflating an air mattress in front of the fireplace while having an intense conversation.

"—bills in your name!" Joe said in exasperation.

"She wouldn't do that," Sam replied in an angry voice. "Someone is trying to steal my identity."

Joe was talking to Sam about the call from the debt collector. To give them privacy, I went to check on Gillian in the guest room.

Gillian met me with suspicion, barely cracking the door open, and assured me she was fine.

Just before eleven, everyone was settling down for a quiet night. Sam, Ernie, Becky, and Helene, who elected to camp in the game room, were watching a movie. Luke joined them.

I was with Joe in the living room, relaxing on the air mattress, when the electricity failed. We were plunged into darkness. I swore in frustration. *What else could go wrong?*

Joe pulled me to his side. "Relax. It's just a power outage. Let's break out the candles."

Joe and I felt our way across the room to retrieve the candles and flashlights we kept stored inside the hutch. As we lit candles, Gillian appeared in the doorway, moving by the light of her phone.

"Could I have a candle, Eleanor?" Gillian asked.

Restraining uncharitable thoughts, I forced myself to be friendly. "Here's one," I said in a polite voice, handing her a cinnamon-scented jar candle.

"Thank you," she said. "Goodnight."

Luke hobbled in. "My leg is aching, and I need a flashlight." He sank into the chocolate-colored couch and placed a pillow under his leg.

Joe and I distributed candles and matches to the bathrooms. The game room crowd was wide awake, so we left them the camping lantern and board games.

Back in the living room, Luke was uncharacteristically cranky, lying on the couch with a strained look on his face. "I took my pain medicine, but my ankle is throbbing."

I tried to distract him from his aching leg. "We have logs for the fireplace. We can light a fire to keep warm, and I can make hot chocolate on the gas stove if I light it manually."

"Can you?" Luke asked with relief. "That would be great."

Becky and Ernie appeared in the doorway. "Hot chocolate? Sounds wonderful," said Becky.

Joe ignited the logs while I went to make a large batch of hot chocolate. After distributing the beverages with marshmallows, I climbed onto the air mattress with Joe. We sat with Luke, watching the flames dance and sipping hot chocolate.

Finishing my drink, I asked, "Is it midnight yet?"

"Yes," said Joe. "Why?"

"The Baby Jesus is still covered in the Nativity scene. I get to unwrap him!" I jumped up and picked up the wrapped figure from the hutch near the fireplace.

"Why not wait until morning?" my husband said, rising from the mattress and walking to the Nativity display.

But I had the cloth halfway unwrapped already. Then, a glittery object fell from the wrapping. "Oh, my! I think I found it!" I picked up the bracelet from where it had fallen on the hutch.

"Is that Gillian's bracelet?" Luke asked, squinting in the flickering light.

"Yes," Joe said.

"Did it fall into the Nativity?" Luke asked.

"No. Someone wrapped it inside the cloth with the figurine," I said in a shocked whisper. "We need to give it back to Gillian."

"Someone hid it 'away in a manger'?" Luke asked incredulously.

"Who did this?" Horrified, I turned to Joe and shivered in the cold. "Everyone knew the baby in the manger wouldn't be unwrapped until Christmas."

"I don't know, Eleanor. But I have an idea." Joe took the bracelet from my hand. "I'm putting this back. In the morning, we'll see who unwraps it. The thief probably planned to retrieve it. Maybe Gillian put it there herself."

"What if whoever unwraps it is shocked and announces it?" I said. "We still wouldn't know who hid it." I worried Sam had done it. He had the opportunity to hide the bracelet, and he had a motive if the bill collector calling him was indicative of his financial status. He'd been in the room alone, supposedly depositing presents under the tree. Or was the thief Ernie, the laconic Louisianan who suddenly bought jewelry for Becky in spite of his own financial difficulties? Or even Becky, who loved gemstones but claimed she didn't notice the bracelet? I swallowed hard, remembering Becky and Helene bent over the Nativity, searching it earlier.

"We'll figure this out in the morning." Joe said after replacing the bracelet in the Nativity. "Let's get some sleep."

Luke decided to sleep on the couch. With the power out, the fireplace made the living room warmer than the master bedroom. Before long, Luke's breathing became heavy and even, and the laughter in the game room died down. I blew out the candles, dripped the faucets, and went to sleep next to Joe on the air mattress as sleet pelted the house.

* * * *

I awoke, shivering, in the gray, pre-dawn light. Luke and Joe were asleep, and the electricity was still out, but I could hear movement. Someone was up, probably going to the bathroom. I rose to look out the window at our white Christmas. Icicles hung from the roof. Ice encased tree branches. The yard was a bumpy white patch.

I sensed movement in the doorway as I turned away from the window, but no one was there. *Was that the thief?* I rushed to the hall, but it was empty.

Grabbing a book and a blanket, I settled down to keep watch until the others awoke.

An hour later, Joe and Luke woke up.

I whispered. "I have to make breakfast, so I can't guard the Nativity. You'll have to keep watch."

"I can watch, but if I have to chase somebody, I'm useless," Luke said.

Ernie and Becky entered the living room.

"What do you mean you're useless?" Becky called, hearing the end of his comment. "Are you whining about your foot? You weren't that useful with two good feet." Becky enjoyed teasing her brothers.

Luke stuck his tongue out at her.

Becky turned to me. "Merry Christmas, Eleanor. We came to help with breakfast."

I watched as Becky crossed the room, hoping she wasn't approaching the Nativity. She stopped by the Christmas tree and stared out the window at the ice. I breathed a sigh of relief. "Merry Christmas to you, too. You can help set the table." I paused as she moved toward the fireplace. "Is Gillian up yet?"

A voice from the entryway behind me said, "I'm here." Gillian stood fully dressed for the cold, clutching her purse.

"Are you going somewhere?" Joe asked.

She waved her cell phone. "I ordered a ride. It should be here in thirty minutes. I won't stay here in this freezing cold house with thieves."

Luke and Becky rolled their eyes in sibling unison.

"I'm sorry you feel that way," I said, suppressing my indignation as I realized that she was right. Someone hid her bracelet, and we needed to return it to her before her car arrived. I shot Joe a look of concern.

He nodded understanding.

"Excuse me." I retreated to the kitchen.

After lighting the stove, starting coffee, and scrambling eggs, I returned to the living room, leaving Becky to slice a loaf of cinnamon pumpkin bread and to direct Ernie as he set the table. Sam was exiting the living room as I arrived. He appeared aggravated, his tumultuous expression at odds with his cheerful sweater. His farewell discussion with Gillian obviously hadn't gone well. I peeked at Joe, who gave me a quick shake of his head indicating no new developments.

As Gillian stood playing with her phone, I gave Joe a look of desperation. We needed to get her bracelet back to her.

Joe read my look and said, "Gillian, the Baby Jesus is still wrapped in our Nativity scene. Would you care to uncover him? It's a family tradition." He spoke to her warmly, with kindness in his voice, trying to put her at ease.

I held my breath wondering if Gillian would explode when she found her bracelet. I wanted to apologize to Gillian, but, as I opened my mouth, Joe shot me a quelling look, so I swallowed my words.

Gillian stared at Joe suspiciously for a moment. "Okay." She strolled to the Nativity scene and bent over it for a few beats too long. When she straightened, she held the Baby in her right hand. Its cloth covering hid her left hand. She swaddled the figure carefully, head now uncovered, and replaced it in the manger.

A honking horn announced a car's arrival.

Gillian faced Joe and me with an air of caution, backing toward the door as if she were afraid of attack. "That's my ride. I'll be in touch through my attorney. You are liable for the loss of my bracelet on your property. If you don't find my bracelet and return it to me, I'll file a claim against your homeowner's insurance. Merry Christmas." She rushed toward the door, but stopped when Joe blocked her.

Luke hobbled over behind Gillian.

Joe asked, "What did you put in your pocket?"

"I don't know what game you're playing, but I'm done." Her cheeks flushed. "My ride is waiting. I won't be held hostage!" Gillian tried to sidestep Joe. Realizing she couldn't get past him, she swung around and found Luke behind her. Gillian kicked wildly at Luke's crutches, knocking one away. Luke stood balancing on the other crutch, obstructing her path. Gillian uttered an enraged shriek and grabbed the dropped crutch. She began swinging it like a club at Joe and Luke. They ducked to dodge blows. As I tried to grab the crutch, one wild swing knocked a painting from the wall.

Sam raced into the room. He grabbed Gillian's arms and pinned them. "What is going on? Stop that!"

A knock sounded at the door, and I hurried to open it. Through the front window I'd observed another car arriving. At the door stood a police detective with his badge clipped to his belt.

"Come in, detective. You can settle a problem for us," I said.

Gillian's reddened nose flared at the sight of the detective, then she burst into tears. "I can't talk right now. I'm too upset. I won't stay near these horrible people!" She shook free of Sam and tried to bypass the detective.

"Don't let her go! Her supposedly missing bracelet is in her pocket," I yelled.

The detective filled the doorway and said, "One moment, ma'am. I'm here about a missing fifty-thousand-dollar bracelet. If it was found, I'd like to discuss it."

Gillian scowled at me, shooting daggers with her eyes.

Hearing the commotion, the rest of the guests entered the room.

I said, "Breakfast is ready, y'all. Joe, Sam, Luke, and Gillian need to talk to this detective, but the rest of us can eat. Come to the table."

* * * *

Over breakfast, I explained how I had found the bracelet and I theorized about Gillian's scheme. "She must have slipped the bracelet off before passing through the kitchen and dropped a stone onto the cake as 'proof' of the theft, before hiding the bracelet in the Nativity. Then, she joined Sam by the Christmas tree. Gillian planned to retrieve the bracelet before leaving last night, knowing we wouldn't unwrap the Baby Jesus figure until today. The ice storm interfered with her plan." I mulled over my logic, feeling something wasn't quite right.

Helene's face lit with anger. "I searched the Nativity! But I didn't unwrap the Baby Jesus. I was looking to see if something fell between the figures, not searching for something intentionally hidden. She probably counted on that. Eleanor, did she want someone arrested for theft?"

I shook my head. "When she tried to leave, she said we were liable for her loss. The police wouldn't have sufficient evidence for an arrest, but Gillian could prove that her 'loss' occurred in our house, on our property. She could use the police report to file a claim against our homeowner's insurance, hoping the company paid off or settled out of court if she threatened a lawsuit. She's a con artist."

Helene grimaced in disgust. "If you hadn't found the bracelet last night, you might have torn the house apart searching and never found the bracelet. We might have suspected each other forever. That sadistic witch!"

After the detective left, Joe, Sam, and Luke joined us in the dining room.

"Did the detective arrest Gillian?" Becky asked hopefully.

"No," Luke said as he swung into the room. "She told him she found the bracelet accidentally and tried to leave since she didn't know who the thief was. She said she was scared of us."

Joe sat next to me at the table. "The detective didn't believe her, especially since she has a criminal record for opening credit accounts in other peoples' names. But he couldn't prove she was lying. He decided to let everyone walk away and call it 'case closed.'"

Luke propped his crutches against the wall and sank into a chair at the table. "At least a report will be on file. If Gillian tries this again, the record will show that she's played this reindeer game before."

As we all groaned at Luke, Sam cleared his throat.

All eyes turned to Sam, who was standing next to the table in his tacky Christmas sweater, shoulders down and head low with a sheepish expression. "I'm so sorry everyone. I didn't know she was like that."

I said, "Sam, you have terrible taste in girlfriends, but we love you anyway."

Sam gave me a sheepish grin and said he needed coffee.

While Helene, Ernie, and Sam crossed to the kitchen to get coffee, I glanced up from my food with a nagging thought that I had missed something. Why was a jewel in the cake where someone might swallow it? I looked toward the kitchen and watched my husband and his siblings laughing together. Why didn't Gillian collect the bracelet without having to be prodded to go to the Nativity? Then, the missing puzzle pieces clicked into place in my brain. I remembered that debt collection call. Joe's argument with Sam over the debt became clearer once I knew Gillian had a criminal record for opening accounts in other people's names.

Joe had argued with Sam more than once. If Joe knew Gillian was spending money in Sam's name, but Sam wouldn't believe it, what steps would Joe take to protect his younger brother?

First, he would enlist his siblings for help.

Becky's red hair caught my eye. She had played the outraged, fiery-tempered, red-head all evening, and she lied about seeing the bracelet. Pretending not to notice it on Gillian's wrist rang false to me.

Luke laughed at something Becky said, and I turned my attention to him. He was a known prankster and the only one who sat next to Gillian around the time the bracelet vanished. He could have taken the bracelet from Gillian's wrist and given it to Becky, who hid it, possibly while pretending to search the Nativity.

If Luke had the bracelet first, that explained the jewel on the cake. Luke must have placed one jewel on his own cake slice, a nice touch to agitate Gillian into further accusations and embarrass Sam. It also pried Gillian from Sam's side for the night.

Finally, Joe stopped me from giving the bracelet back to Gillian and arranged for Gillian to find the bracelet. Because she was a crook, she'd tried to walk out quietly with the bracelet, making her look even guiltier. Joe, Becky, and Luke had made Sam see Gillian at her worst, and Gillian had unknowingly helped them. They'd set Gillian up, scamming the scammer in order to detach her from their brother.

As for Gillian's behavior: if she hadn't been devious, she'd have announced that she found the bracelet. Instead, she chose to say nothing, intending to take revenge by filing an insurance claim. She was a rotten person, but she was right about the conspiracy against her.

I gave Becky, Luke, and Joe a hard, accusatory frown as they returned to the table. Becky and Luke flinched, turning embarrassed faces to their food. I stared at Joe, who came and put an arm around me.

I stiffened in annoyance.

My husband leaned into me and whispered softly in my ear, "We apologize. I noticed the storm coming early. Becky noticed the bracelet. Luke has a gift for complex pranks. We cooked up a scheme while Sam showed Gillian the house. I knew we probably couldn't fool you entirely, but you were distracted with the dinner preparations. We almost cracked when Gillian called the police, but we took the chance of seeing the plan through to the end. You must have figured out why we did it. Forgive us, Eleanor?"

I bit my lip, peeved with them all, and whispered furiously, "This scheme could have exploded in your faces in twenty different ways! And you ruined my Christmas Eve dinner!" I closed my eyes for a moment. "But you did disentangle Sam from Gillian, so I might forgive you eventually." After all, I'd married him because he cared so much for other people, especially his family. I thought I knew my husband, but I hadn't understood how far he would go to protect the ones he loved, even from themselves. We would have to discuss this in depth, but now was not the time for it. I'd need time to process this revelation.

Joe gave me an apologetic kiss belied by the mischievous twinkle in his eye. As Helene, Ernie, and Sam returned to the table with fresh coffee, Joe raised his coffee mug, "Merry Christmas, everyone! Here's to family!"

N.M. Cedeño (nmcedeno.com) writes mystery short stories and novels that vary from traditional to romantic suspense and from paranormal to science fiction. She is a member of Sisters in Crime and its Heart of Texas Chapter, where she has served as chapter vice president and president. She is a member of the Short Mystery Fiction Society. Ms. Cedeño blogs with several other Heart of Texas mystery writers at InkStainedWretches.home.blog.

TOO YOUNG TO DIE

ELIZABETH ZELVIN

The only way to get a top-floor ocean-view apartment at Breezy Shores, "the friendliest active senior community in Palm Beach County," is to wait till one of your friends drops dead. I was cozy enough in my second-floor two-bedroom rental facing the parking lot. The price was right, leaving enough in my virtual piggy bank to go shopping on Worth Avenue in Palm Beach and lose a few bucks to my best friend Lucille and the rowdy gang of octogenarian widows whose daily company kept my heart open and my ribs sore from laughing. But I coveted Lucille's fabulous eyrie with its balcony overlooking the horizon from the moment I crossed the threshold for my first game of poker with the girls.

Lucille spotted me at poolside shortly after I moved in. She plumped her zaftig five foot one, draped in yards of fluttering magenta caftan and augmented by matching three-inch mules and towering turban, in the chaise longue next to mine.

"Shoo me away if you don't want company," she said. "I'm Lucille Shaw."

"No, please, I'm delighted," I said. "Harriet Lipsky."

She eyed my black straw hat and black bikini.

"New widow?"

"Is it that obvious? I try not to look morose. But it's only been six months, and I miss my husband."

"I felt the same when Jack died," Lucille said, "but it's been five years now. You're lucky you can still wear a bikini."

Most women around here asked, "Have you had work done?"

The way my skin still wrapped tight around my bones came free, thanks to my dad's height and my mother's wrinkle-proof skin. I stood six foot three before age started trying to make a little old lady of me. I wasn't going gently.

Lucille asked, "Do you play poker?"

"Some," I said warily.

"You must meet the girls," she said. "We're all widows. We meet for lunch and poker on my balcony three times a week. It's very informal. We have only a couple of rules. We don't call ourselves 'girls' where anyone else can hear. And we never say 'passed away.' When we talk about death and dying, we say 'dead' and 'died.'"

"So far, so good. Anything else?"

"No jacks wild."

You can tell a lot about a woman at the poker table.

The first time we played, Lucille, seated on my left, caught me staring at Sharon, who wore a rock the size of Gibraltar—an emerald set in a pendant dripping with diamonds. Lucille whispered in my bad ear, but even with the high-tech hearing aid, I missed it.

"Change places with me and say it again." I resettled myself and pointed to my good ear.

"Her first husband was a jeweler," Lucille said. "We're mirror twins—my other ear's the bad one. When she drinks, she loses. If she loses enough, she bets the Rock."

"You let her?"

"Shh, keep your voice down. She insists."

"Would you keep it if you won it?"

Adele, on Lucille's right, said, "In some situations, scruples are overrated."

Annette, pouting, said across the table, "That from the woman who retired with a bundle after forty years in corporate law."

Charlotte, on my left, said, "Diamonds are overrated, but I wouldn't turn up my nose at an emerald." Doyenne of the group at eighty-nine, she was my favorite along with Lucille. "Anyhow, she's managed never to lose it."

"Why are we talking?" Sharon, frowning at her hand, hadn't heard a word. "Let's play poker."

Lucille and I, diving simultaneously for our cards, got in each other's way and cracked our funny bones together. Then we dug each other in the ribs and giggled.

Lucille bet the apartment only once. Annette, who had family in France, came back from a visit bearing great wine and cheeses, along with foie gras from Toulouse. Lucille supplied the best baguettes in West Palm Beach. We all ate and drank a lot and became extremely silly. I was the big winner that night and already grinning like a Cheshire cat because I'd scored three bottles of Château Pichon Lalande 2016 from Annette and a stunning pair of sterling silver Art Deco earrings from Sharon. Lucille won a much more valuable pair of earrings off Sharon, sapphire studs. Adele had bad hands all night, and Charlotte dropped out too, saying forget poker, she hadn't tasted Coulommiers this good since her honeymoon in 1959. Only Lucille and I were left.

I was about to say, "Let's call it quits."

"Let's play one more hand," Lucille said. "Adele, write this down in lawyer language. In the event of my death, I, Lucille Shaw, hereby bequeath my apartment and all its contents to my dear friend Harriet Lipsky. I'll sign it. Why not, Harriet? You fell in love with my apartment at first sight. Your place is too small, and it's a rental. What if you lost it?"

"Don't be silly, Lucille," I said.

"Don't be morbid, Lucille," Sharon said.

"*Oh-là-là*!" Annette said. "We all love your apartment."

"You don't need it. Harriet does."

"No, I don't," I said. "I forbid you to die to upgrade my housing. You're only eighty-four—way too young to die."

"We're all too young to die," Charlotte said.

"Who says you're going to win this hand, anyway?" Lucille said. "Go on, Adele, write it down. And make sure it's legal."

"If you must, you madwoman," I said. "I love you, Lucille, win or lose."

I took two cards.

Lucille took one.

"I'm all in," she said.

"No, Lucille, don't bet the sapphires," I said. "They match your eyes."

Lucille scooped up the earrings, pushed the rest of her pot forward, and laid down a full house of tens and jacks.

I had three queens and two aces.

"Don't let my family see this IOU, Harriet," Lucille said as she handed the paper over. "They'd kill for my apartment."

"I won't let them," I said. "I'm going to live another quarter century." None of us said "forever" anymore.

"They won't kill you," Adele said. "They'll kill Lucille and sue the blood out of your veins."

I wore the Art Deco earrings, put the Bordeaux away to age till 2026, and tacked Lucille's IOU on the bulletin board in my kitchen as a good joke.

Breezy Shores defined "active senior" as anyone over fifty-five who didn't need a caregiver, but Hallie Shaw and her sister Nina barely qualified as seniors. They were the late Jack's nieces, not Lucille's, and I thought both were under sixty even now. Their current apartments were more like mine than Lucille's in scale and location, but since neither was retired or always in residence, that should have been okay.

Lucille insisted I get to know the Shaws once she and I had bonded and I was comfortable with the poker gang. I had heard of Hallie Shaw, the creative force behind *Get It Wright*, the latest contender for TV crime show glory. The Wrights were a married couple, one a cop, the other a journalist—partners cum adversaries—who take on major crimes and, after a series of conflicts, obstacles, and twists, see justice done. I watched it myself and found it clever and fast paced. Hallie was one of the few A-list female showrunners in TV. It was a cut-throat industry, and she looked and sounded like a woman who'd cut her share of throats. I was ready to like her, but I saw her go on guard the moment Lucille introduced me as "my best friend."

"Oh, everyone's Lucille's best friend." Her laugh tinkled like shards of ice.

Lucille was popular, but she wasn't shallow. I knew the accusation hurt. Evidently, so did Hallie.

Hallie's sister Nina was a high-end interior decorator whose thin lips sprayed designer brand names like a dressmaker spitting pins. When I asked what she thought of Lucille's decor, she dismissed the charming patio furniture as "fit for a suburban rumpus room" and sneered at the "kitschy" golden swan fixtures in Lucille's master bathroom. They were, but they were meant to be a joke. Jack surprised Lucille with them—and a sexy bubble bath, champagne, and flowers rendezvous—on their fiftieth wedding anniversary. They made her chuckle every time she saw them. After he died, that bathroom became her favorite place to cry and remember Jack. There are worse places to mourn the love of your life than in a bubble bath.

Hallie was a big draw among the celebrity buffs at Lucille's famous parties. There were fewer of those than might be expected, because for every year past seventy-five, you give less and less of a damn. People showed up for the pleasure of Lucille's company, her catering, and the ambiance of that fabulous apartment. The whole poker gang pitched in with advice before my first party at Lucille's in what Charlotte called "mixed company"—the Hallie Shaw crowd along with the retirees.

"Make sure you tell them you taught in the South Bronx," Charlotte said.

"*Don't* say you were a schoolteacher," Annette said. "Talk about the places you and Ben traveled, how you climbed Kilimanjaro and went dogsledding and lived in Potosí for six months."

"Wear a little black dress, and I'll lend you the Rock," Sharon said.

"Why don't you just bring your latest bank statement?" Adele said drily.

"Don't be silly," I said. "It's a party at Lucille's, not the Oscars. I was the tallest person in the room when I was twelve years old. I don't like being conspicuous."

"Wear whatever you like," Lucille said, "and be yourself. The whole point is to have fun."

"Then stay away from the terrible two," Adele said. "I suppose they're coming?"

"They're not that bad," Lucille said. "She means Hallie's daughters, Priscilla and Prunella. They're only kids."

"Feral post-adolescents," Charlotte said, "with tongues as sharp as sushi knives. Will the drug-addicted brother be there?"

"Don't be mean," Lucille said. "He's in rehab in Delray Beach and doing very well. Sharon, wear the Rock yourself. Just for fun."

Hallie's daughters didn't scare me. I had sixty years on them and wasn't sushi. They were easy to spot at the party. The taller one had Snow White coloring—skin white as snow, hair black as ebony—and an expression more like Grumpy's. The other was a Cinderella, blond with ashen highlights, wearing the artful kind of rags that cost a fortune on Worth Avenue. I pretended not to see Lucille trying to beckon me over to meet them. When that didn't work, I shook my head vehemently.

"Priss, Prune, I did want you to meet my friend Harriet. See the tall woman by the window? Maybe later."

"Who *is* she?" Snow White yawned, not concerned that I was within earshot.

"She's my best friend," Lucille said.

"Get it right, Priss," Cinderella said. "Be nice to Aunt Lu."

"Fuck you, Prune," Priss said without heat. "You get it right. You go pet the giraffe."

"Never mind," Lucille snapped. "I'll tell her not to waste her time on you."

I went to meet her as they drifted away.

"Back to the zoo," I said cheerfully. "Don't let them get to you."

"It's my party and I'll cry if I want to," she said. "With Jack gone, those predatory little wretches are the closest I have to family."

"Families are overrated," I said. "I imagine God saying wistfully, 'It was such a good idea!'"

The rest of the party was pleasant. All the other guests were friendly. I had intelligent conversations with several neighbors I'd never before seen vertical and fully clothed. I let a sixtyish gentleman named Murray tell me how much lessons at Fred Astaire would improve my posture and "loosen up the kinks." I flirted for the first time in decades with a delightful young man named Jason who made me forget my age completely for ten minutes. Flirting is a grand restorative, much better than cucumber slices on the eyes or a mud bath at an expensive spa.

The easy life at Breezy Shores rolled on. We played poker. I bought a purple bathing suit. We all got Kindles and read a lot of books down at the pool. Sharon lost a ring at the Miami Opera and went out for dinner with the widower who found it for her. Hallie made friends with Adele, because Priss was applying to law school. Nina, who adored New York, thawed a bit on learning I remembered long-gone temples to good food on the Upper West Side, like Lichtman's where they had the poppy-seed strudel and Williams where they had the best gefilte fish. We almost had a decent conversation. If twenty-first century medicine and alternative health and wellness weren't quite the Fountain of Youth, they kept us sharp and sassy. But they didn't help Lucille on the bright morning when Lucille's cleaning lady found her lying on her bed, her blood and brains staining the quilted satin comforter and a .22 pistol in her hand.

Alpharita behaved appropriately in the circumstances, in my opinion. She was careful not to approach the bed or touch anything. As she told me and, later, the police, she only screamed once and cried very briefly. Then she raced down to the second floor and pounded on my door.

"Ms. Harriet! You've got to come *now!*"

Lucille always consulted me when three were needed to address a problem. Along with Alpharita, we had dealt with the exploding microwave, the mouse in the box spring in the back guest room, and the patio furniture set with "some assembly required." I knew that this wasn't a mouse.

I threw my cell phone into the pocket of my lounge pajamas, thrust my bare feet into a pair of slippers, grabbed my keys, and scurried after Alpharita.

"What happened? Is she okay? Do we need to call a doctor?"

"You have to see for yourself."

I stopped short in Lucille's doorway. Grasping Alpharita's thin wrist, I pulled her back and got an arm around her shoulders. She was shivering. So was I.

"You're in shock," I said. "Let's not touch anything. I'm going to call nine-one-one now. We have to stay calm."

"Why would she kill herself, Ms. Harriet?" Alpharita asked. "Did she have bad news? Lose someone she loved, maybe?"

Good question. I could hardly bear to look at the figure on the bed. The patio doors were locked, and the little handgun lay where it had fallen from her slack fingers.

If the police wanted to see my ID, I'd have to take them back to my apartment. It was a mess. Unmade bed. Dishes in the sink. Bulletin board studded with supermarket coupons, photos of the poker gang, and that scrap of paper saying I got Lucille's apartment if she died.

"Alpharita. Did the concierge see you come in?"

"We said good morning," she said. "Ten minutes before I knocked on your door."

Once I steeled myself to look at poor Lucille, I couldn't look away. Her shattered head would give me nightmares. I took photos with my phone while we waited, a compromise between reality and distance. Whether I would ever be able to look at them was another story. I was glad that I'd told Lucille I loved her.

The police escorted me to my apartment right away. No fascinating glimpses of crime scene investigation. I felt shaky enough to be relieved. They didn't even glance at my bulletin board. I identified myself as a close friend who'd known Lucille for less than a year. When they asked if I could tell them her next of kin, I told them about Hallie Shaw, saying she was a Breezy Shores resident but an in-law, not a blood relative.

"Lucille's well organized," I said. "I'm sure you'll find her lawyer's name in her address book. Her iPhone, and she also has a Rolodex."

He didn't look old enough to know what a Rolodex was.

The next night was our regular poker night. We met at my place. I'd baked three kinds of cookies and stocked up on alcohol.

"We're not playing poker, are we?" Charlotte said.

"Of course not," Sharon said. "It's Lucille's wake."

"*Incroyable*!" Annette said. She eased the cork out of a bottle of prosecco without a pop. "Something must have been terribly wrong."

"A gun!" Charlotte shuddered. "Messy! Lucille was always so well put together."

"If she'd taken a bottle of Xanax and a bottle of Grey Goose," Sharon said, "and slipped away in her bath surrounded by candles and lilies, that I could have understood."

"She didn't take Xanax anymore," Adele said, "not since she went to family week at the nephew's rehab in Delray Beach."

"That doesn't excuse her shooting herself in the head and leaving us all traumatized!" Charlotte's lip trembled.

"Harriet's the only one who went through a real trauma," Adele said.

"Too bad not one of us is a *psy*," Annette said. "A shrink."

"If you need a lawyer, Harriet," Adele said, "I'm there for you."

"I don't need a lawyer or a shrink," I said.

"You found the body," Sharon said. "Our fingerprints, *all* our fingerprints, are all over that apartment."

"Not the way Alpharita cleans," Charlotte said.

"I didn't cross the threshold," I said.

Sharon snickered. Too much prosecco.

"Like a vampire."

"You're the heir to that apartment, sweetie," Adele said. "Do you still have the document I drew up?"

"Yes," I said. "But it was a joke."

"When I execute a document," Adele said, "it's not a joke. It's a legal instrument."

"The Shaws won't like that," I said. "Can't I just tear it up?"

"No!" they chorused.

"It will hold up in court if it gets that far," Adele assured me. "What do you think that apartment is worth?" she said. "A million? Two million? You can't keep it a secret."

Lucille's lawyer, Nancy Vesey, agreed. She called the next morning, suggesting we meet as soon as possible. Lucille had bequeathed me the apartment in a codicil to her will and left me enough money in trust to pay the maintenance and then some. I could redecorate the place from top to bottom if I felt like it. I could afford to dine in the three-star restaurant on the ground floor overlooking the ocean whenever I wanted, if I was willing to spend my mornings in the four-star health club working it off. When I died, it would all revert to the Shaws. Except if my death was suspicious in any way, it went to her favorite charities. Hallie and Nina would love that clause. I quailed at the thought of meeting them after they heard about it.

"Did she have to say that?" I asked Nancy. "I meet these people at the pool with nothing but a bikini between me and the evil eye."

"Lucille insisted. She said she wanted them to behave."

I liked the lawyer, a perky young woman in her forties with a curly smile like a dolphin's. We'd be seeing a lot of each other, as we'd been named co-executors of Lucille's estate.

"I'll file the papers and deal with the authorities," she said. "And I'll break the news to the Shaws that they're not executors."

"Thank you," I said. "I don't think Hallie or Nina will take it well."

"They should," Nancy said, the dolphin smile stretching till it looked more like a shark's. "What Lucille left you is a drop in the bucket to what the two of them are getting."

"They may not see it that way," I said. "They may want to move in. Can you have the locks changed immediately and tell them it's routine? In fact, do they have to know I'm co-executor?"

"If they challenge you, we tell the truth," Nancy said. "Lucille's affairs are your business. You can go through all the stuff in her apartment. And keep track of your hours. They're billable to the estate."

I felt more comfortable dealing with the various jurisdictions involved in Lucille's suspicious death as co-executor of her estate than as a potential suspect. I'd met the local town police when I called 911. The Palm Beach County medical examiner's office did an autopsy—something I didn't want to think about too closely—and a death investigator ruled the death a suicide. On that basis, the homicide unit from the county sheriff's office declined to get involved, though a deputy came and asked me a few questions.

I had never understood why Lucille insisted on giving me her apartment. It made more sense when we learned that she was already thinking about dying. The autopsy uncovered the reason: Lucille had leukemia. She hadn't told anyone. As executor, I had to go through her papers to find the oncologist and confirm that she'd been told her diagnosis. That was enough for the police.

I asked about the gun. They didn't even try to trace it. Saturday night specials were easy to obtain in Florida. It was a "girly" gun—the detective's word, not mine—and had no one's fingerprints on it except Lucille's.

"Leukemia!" Charlotte said. "What type of leukemia? My second husband had it for ages. His wasn't aggressive at all. He got his diagnosis when he was thirty-six, and he lived another twenty years."

"He must have been sick, though," Sharon said. "Did he get chemo?"

"Chemo and radiation," Charlotte said, "six times, and it was terrible. But he had five remissions, too, and we were very happy during those periods. He didn't just give up."

"I don't think Lucille would have given up either," I said. "She would have fought."

"She'd just found out," Annette said. "She might have been depressed."

"She saw a lawyer and put her affairs in order," Adele said. "It's something people do when they know they *might* die."

"Be glad they're sure she killed herself," Sharon said. "Harriet benefits by her death."

"Don't be mean, Sharon," Charlotte said. "Harriet loved Lucille."

"I'm just saying."

"The Shaws benefit too," Adele said.

"It's not fair," Sharon said. "The Shaws are loaded."

"Get it right, as Priss and Prune say," Annette said. "Hallie is loaded. Her show is syndicated, and it will run forever. Nina's business, who knows? It could be all, *comme on dit*, window dressing."

"I have to meet them at the lawyer's," I said. "I'm not looking forward to it."

"Lucille did leave you the place 'and contents,' didn't she?" Annette said.

"It isn't mine yet," I said. "Nancy Vesey took me to lunch and told me horror stories about Florida probate court. Besides, Jack's family has a point. It was a poker game, for God's sake."

"In the meantime," Sharon said, "think about the view and our lovely lunches. If we all live to a hundred, think how many extra years of pleasure you'll be giving the rest of us."

"She wanted you to have it," Adele said.

I pinched the bridge of my nose between my thumb and forefinger.

"Enough, you flock of harpies," Charlotte said. "We're giving Harriet a migraine."

"I'm going to ask the Shaws to plan the funeral," I said. "If they feel they're in charge, they'll be easier to deal with, so please don't make a fuss."

I wasn't sure the family would want the responsibility. But Hallie and Nina took control. If they hadn't, I'd have given Lucille the kind of send-off she'd have enjoyed. They opted for a minimal funeral service. No chance for Lucille's friends to get up and eulogize her with those sulky faces in the first row. The residents of Breezy Shores turned out in force anyway. Everyone had liked Lucille. Young people who'd known her from her volunteer work showed up too. I spotted the young man I'd flirted with at her party. He winked and raised a finger to his lips.

I sat behind Priss and Prune, who didn't stop sniping and grumbling for a moment.

"Young people shouldn't have to go to funerals."

"She didn't leave anything to *us*, so why do we have to be here?"

"Too bad Great-Aunt Lu didn't get it right. She should have left us the apartment. Or she could have left it to the baby to live in between rehabs."

"Shh, we're not supposed to talk about him."

After that, I was very surprised to receive an invitation from Hallie to a poolside brunch, ostensibly to meet a famous actor who'd recently been a guest star on *Get It Wright*. I enjoyed my fifteen seconds of exposure to the twinkling eyes and perfect teeth. The brief contact convinced me that "star quality" is more than a myth. I didn't enjoy being introduced as "my ancient late Step-aunt Lucille's heir along with me and Nina. Dear Uncle Jack had the most marvelous collection of *objets*."

"Collections," Nina said.

"Get it right, Ma," Prune muttered.

"Oh, yes," Hallie said. "Cameos. Paul Revere dollhouse furniture. I remember playing with them when I was little."

"She was never little," Priss said behind her hand.

Nina's eyes lit up. "Netsuke. Snuffboxes."

Objets my foot. Those fidgety collectibles were long gone. When you lost the love of your life, you wanted to hang onto your memories, not all their stuff. Especially stuff that required dusting and didn't particularly interest you. I said so as politely as I could as soon as the star turned his dazzling smile on someone else.

"I don't believe you," Nina said. "She must have known I'd be the best person to have those things."

"Why didn't you ask her, Neens?" Hallie said. "You spent more time with her than I did."

"What do you mean?" Nina bridled. "I've been in New York on buying trips most of the last six months."

"Then why did your people tell me you were down here," Hallie demanded, "every time I tried to reach you?"

"Yeah, Aunt Nina, get it right," Prune said. "Did you drop in on poor old Great-Aunt Lu to discuss her will?"

"When I called *your* office in LA last week, Hallie," Nina said, "they said you were taking a few days rest with family. But I haven't seen you."

"Since when do you ever rest, Ma?" Priss inquired.

"Enough!" Hallie said.

"Lucille committed suicide," I said firmly.

"Oh, yeah?" Prune said. "Then how come they wouldn't let us cremate her?"

I hadn't known they wanted to. I'd hated the thought of Lucille's ashes in a box, kicking around on a shelf with these awful women making jokes about them. I'd been relieved the Shaws had chosen burial. Did that mean the sheriff's department's decision not to investigate was only provisional? I thought they had to go by the death investigator's finding. I'd asked Nancy. Had someone made a mistake during the autopsy? I needed to look at the photos I'd taken at the scene.

As co-executor of Lucille's estate, I moved into Lucille's place without waiting for probate. I hoped my friends' company would help me through the transition. But the dynamics of the poker gang didn't work anymore.

Adele wanted to play lawyer and advisor to me rather than friend. Charlotte got more frail as her ninetieth birthday approached, though she denied it. Sharon lost interest in poker. She started taking dance classes at Fred Astaire in Palm Beach Gardens. We all suspected she'd met a new man. I hoped it wasn't Murray. Annette took to calling us all *chérie*, as if she couldn't remember our names, and saying *bisou bisou* instead of goodbye.

One evening, I went to open the balcony door wider to let in the breeze off the ocean. Sharon and Annette were on the balcony, their backs to me.

"Why didn't Lucille leave the apartment to me?" Sharon grumbled. "She was my friend first. I knew her *lots* longer. Lucille *knew* I had financial troubles. She promised she'd do something for me after Cheryl died, but she never did. I counted on her, and she didn't come through."

"Oh, *chérie*," Annette said. "To lose a daughter—I know the pain."

The existence and death of Sharon's daughter was news to me. But I was sure that Annette was childless.

"Once Cheryl was dead, Stuart wouldn't give me child support any more. And when I married Bobby, he cut off my alimony too. It wasn't fair! It was hardly even a marriage. Bobby was a croupier in Las Vegas, for God's sake, and it barely lasted six weeks. Then he found out I couldn't sell the jewelry I inherited from Peter, and I realized the jewelry was the only reason he'd married me."

"So the Rock was not yours to wager at poker," Annette said.

"Damn," Sharon said. "I didn't mean to tell you that. You can't tell anyone!"

"You are *très amusante*, *chérie*. Did Lucille know?"

"She promised not to tell."

That night I pulled up my photos of Lucille's death. The ruin of her poor head and face had become no easier to look at. So I focused on her sprawled body, the gun, her hands, the scene as a whole. I knew nothing about forensics—bullet impact, blood spatter. But maybe I'd spot something out of place.

There's a difference between how someone who's shot herself in the head holds the gun and when someone wants to make a murder look like a suicide. I know this from extensive mystery reading. In fiction, some detail is always wrong, so the investigator can say, "Aha! This woman didn't shoot herself." If Lucille was murdered, you'd think whatever mistake the killer made would be spotted by the crime scene experts or in the autopsy.

Who could possibly have killed Lucille, then posed her as a suicide, and *not made any mistakes*? I remembered Sherlock Holmes's line: "Once you eliminate the impossible, whatever remains, however improbable, must be the truth." Suppose I started with the premise that Lucille couldn't possibly have killed herself. It was too out of character. Then the improbable truth must be that the killer had made no mistakes at all. They had to get it right.

Get It Wright—Hallie Shaw's hit TV series. Get it right—the girls' favorite tag line. The title of the *Wright* show was clever. It had several levels of meaning. The main characters were the Wrights. The cop got the case, the reporter got the story. Together, they had to solve the crime and "get it right." On top of that, Hallie herself was known to be a stickler for "getting it right." She insisted on fact-checking every detail of criminal behavior and police procedure on the show. I read that mystery novelists do this, but writers of TV crime shows don't. In real life, local investigators can't get DNA results back in a couple of hours. Crime scene investigators don't interview witnesses or suspects. Women detectives in the field don't teeter on three-inch heels. Hallie was determined to turn this around on her show. So if anyone knew how to make a homicide look like a genuine suicide, it was she.

But what was her motive? She didn't have to kill for money. *Get It Wright* was a huge success, the latest in a string of them. What else was Hallie, besides a successful showrunner? She was a mother. Why do mothers kill? To protect a child.

It was hard to imagine Hallie Shaw going broody over those self-possessed young monsters, Priscilla and Prunella. It had to be the drug-addicted brother. The one who was in and out of rehab. The one who'd screwed up jobs and relationships and fresh starts his whole life. The one with enablers—people blinded by love and denial who've made excuses, covered up consequences, lied and hoped and rescued and tried again over and over.

How did I know? I'd seen it over and over. And I'd done it myself with a beloved brother. I couldn't help it. If you've ever tried to apply common sense to the unconscious, you'll know how well it works.

Hallie had plenty of money and a belief that she could always get it right. I bet she'd paid for rehab after rehab. But the son had known Mom would always give him another chance, another handout, another parachute. There are a lot of rehabs in South Florida. Hadn't someone mentioned Lucille attending family week? Hallie spent a lot of time shooting her show, promoting it, and doing whatever else she did in New York, LA, and otherwise not in Florida. Suppose she'd asked Lucille to keep an eye on her son.

I googled Hallie Shaw. I should have done it sooner. "The baby" was twenty-seven. His name was Jason. I'd met him twice: at the party, when Lucille herself had told me he was in rehab getting clean, and at the funeral, where his family had been oblivious to his presence. Drunk or sober, my brother had been a charmer. So was Jason. Sneaky, too. No doubt Lucille had been an indulgent and adoring aunt. But she had gone to family week.

A visit to Delray Beach would have taught Lucille about enabling and shown her how to stop. I bet Hallie had never gone to a single family session. She must have realized they'd only tell her to quit rescuing her precious son. She wouldn't have believed that Mom doing nothing was his only chance of beating his addiction. She was used to getting her way.

I guessed there'd been some kind of confrontation when Lucille told Hallie she wouldn't enable Jason anymore and that she'd do all she could to keep Hallie from protecting him from the consequences of his behavior. I doubted either of them had expected violence. I could imagine Hallie losing her temper and snatching up Lucille's gun in the heat of the moment.

"You've got to let him take responsibility for himself," I imagined Lucille saying. "You think you're helping him, but you're killing him."

"I'm killing him! *I'm* killing him!" I imagined Hallie shrieking. She was so controlled that when she lost control, she would lose it thoroughly. "I'll kill *you*!"

I found this scenario convincing, but I had no proof. To go to the authorities, I needed something concrete. I looked through the photos again slowly, thinking hard.

I sometimes get confused between right and left in a photo, thinking it's the same as in a mirror. But I knew on which bedside table in Lucille's bedroom the antique Chinese lamp sat, on which wall the small but genuine Kandinsky hung. Was it possible that Hallie *had* made a mistake?

New premise: It was impossible for anyone, even Hallie Shaw, to fake a suicide without doing *something* wrong. Improbable but true: she'd put Lucille's gun in the *wrong hand.*

How would she know which was Lucille's dominant hand? How would anyone know? I'd had aunts and uncles myself. I'd been fond of them, but did I know their dominant hand? No. Hallie didn't pay Lucille that much attention. The gun was in Lucille's right hand. The setup was perfect—for a right-handed suicide.

But I knew that Lucille was left-handed. We'd gotten in the habit of sitting together, me on the left and Lucille on the right, to accommodate my bad left ear and Lucille's bad right ear, at group meals as well as playing poker. So I constantly saw her pick up and manipulate both cards and utensils using her left hand as the dominant one. I might be the only one who'd noticed.

Nowadays an autopsy wouldn't reveal handedness. In my youth, when people used pens all the time, the middle finger of the writing hand had a bump, often stained with ink. But now, there'd be no way to tell.

Maybe Priss and Prune would be nicer people when they were in their eighties. Or sooner. Maybe the trauma of Mom's arrest would be a wakeup call. Maybe Jason would get clean for real. The three of them would grow closer with Mom in prison and no longer such a star they couldn't compete. I bet she always hounded them to get it right, and in her eyes they always fell short. Maybe they'd get into therapy. Maybe the lightbulb would *really want* to change. If you eliminate the impossible. . . .

Elizabeth Zelvin's short stories appear in *Ellery Queen's Mystery Magazine* and *Alfred Hitchcock's Mystery Magazine* as well as *Black Cat Mystery Magazine* and *Jewish Noir II* (2022). Author of the Bruce Kohler Mysteries and the Mendoza Family Saga, Liz has been nominated three times each for the Derringer and Agatha awards. She considers herself too old to die young but is not an octogenarian yet and just a kid by nonagenarian and centenarian standards.

TO CATCH A PURR-PETRATOR

STACY WOODSON

I think the first week of my summer internship as a production assistant on the Pet Shopping Network is going pretty well until I find the on-air-talent for all things feline face down in a bag of kitty kibble.

I stare at the dark soles of her leopard-print ballet flats, remnants of the price tag's adhesive from the discount store still stuck to the bottom. A half-caf, soy double-shot latte, extra sweet, pools on the floor next to her. The way she's laid out, it reminds me of Cabo, spring break, and when I found my roommate face down with a bottle of tequila.

I step closer, smell the amaretto.

Yup. She's drunk. Just like Wendy.

I shake my head. I've had to do some crazy things for Kat since I started working here, but sobering her up will be a new one.

"Kat." I wonder if she hears me over the grind from the table saw. Long plastic sheets hang from the ceiling and divide our set from the rest of the building. The station manager shifted some of our programming to our sister studio to accommodate the renovation but not for our show. Work stops when Kat goes on the air.

I try again, but she still doesn't move.

Then it hits me. What if she isn't drunk?

What if she's...I swallow....*dead.*

Oh God.

I should do something—CPR, the Heimlich maneuver, one of those first aid thingies. At least check her pulse. I lean forward, wrinkle my nose, blindly reach.

And...

I can't do it.

There are some things even I'm not equipped to deal with. I stand, smooth my skirt, and key my walkie. "We have a..." I pause, a week of walkie protocol swirling through my head.

I can't say there's a stiff in the kibble. Can I?

I'm still debating, when something grips my ankle.

I scream—horror-movie style. I yank my leg back. Kat reaches for me again. This time I see her face. *Swollen. Hives.* I gasp. Something no facial can fix.

"Call an ambulance," Kat wheezes. "Sabrina tried to poison me."

"Coffee Cart Sabrina?" I stare at her in disbelief.

"Make the call, Mindy."

I pull out my phone, call 911 and tell the dispatcher someone tried to poison Kat McMahon.

People are running onto the set now. Some from the loading dock, others from the remodel—sawdust from their shoes littering the floor like confetti. I guess my scream really was loud. Maybe voiceover work is my true calling.

"Chair," Kat squeaks.

"Are you sure you're up to it?"

She nods, eyes on the growing crowd.

I help her to her feet. She weaves, and we both nearly tumble to the floor. At first, I think someone will help us. But no one moves. I guess I can't blame them. On-air-Kat is kind and vibrant. But off-air-Kat is ruthless, especially when it comes to getting what she wants. Just a week working here and even I know this. I can't imagine she's made many friends.

We finally make it to the Daily Deal: *A purr-fectly paw-some plywood chair for both human and feline, this Glamour-Puss original can be yours for just twenty easy payments of $9.99.* I wrote the sales pitch this morning hoping to impress her. *Please don't die.* If this internship doesn't amount to something—a letter of recommendation, a job, *anything*—I'll be back working at my mother's princess party business faster than I can sing "Let it Go."

I line Kat up in front of the chair. She collapses into the seat, raises a hand to her forehead, and groans. "Prop my feet, Mindy."

I glance around and find the canary-colored cat carriers: *portable pet enclosures that let you travel with your favorite cat companion for the hiss-terically low price of $29.99.* I pull one down from the pyramid display and slide it under Kat's feet like an ottoman.

"Pictures," she whispers.

"Why?" I can't imagine Kat wants this moment preserved for posterity.

"Evidence."

I start to tell her to wait for the police. That they will handle these details. But then I remind myself that Kat's approval—her endorsement—is the only thing standing between me and a lifetime wearing that Elsa costume.

I pull out my phone and take pictures of Kat, the spilled coffee. I take one of the gawkers, too: Coffee Cart Sabrina, Canine Cal the Dog Show Host, Paul the Cameraman, Wally the Janitor—who looks like Kris Kringle—and others I don't recognize. I can hear them talking, some about what happened, others about the fantasy football draft. The police and EMS finally arrive too.

"The paramedics are here," I tell Kat.

She peeks up at me. "And Paul?"

"Your…*ex*?" I nod even though I'm still confused why she cares. I step back so the paramedics can work and nearly collide with our station manager in her Marc Jacobs power suit. Blair talks to Kat, but I can't hear what they say because the table saw starts up again.

I bite my lip not sure what to do. Go back to work. Stay. What should an assistant do at a time like this?

"I'm looking for Mindy Budewitz," a police officer yells above the noise. I wave, and he walks over. He's cute in that *Blue Bloods* kind of way.

"You called nine-one-one?"

I nod. I'm distracted by the biceps straining against his sleeves. I wonder how much he can bench-press. I wouldn't mind him bench-pressing me.

He pulls out his notebook, jots something down and yells, "The dispatcher said you mentioned"— the table saw cuts off—"poison."

Poison.

Poison.

The word echoes in the air like a ring announcer said it. No one is talking. No one moves. Everyone is clustered together staring at me over Blue Bloods' shoulder. Even Wally stops sweeping up sawdust and looks at me wide-eyed.

"Ms. Budewitz?"

Wally puts his finger to his lips and shakes his head.

I frown, not sure why he's signaling me to be silent. I stare at the cop, my mind trying to process what's happening. Wally must be warning me about the nondisclosure agreement—the one Blair made me sign, a prerequisite for everyone who works here.

Surely, NDAs don't apply when it comes to attempted murder.

Before I can respond, Blair breezes over. I nearly choke on her perfume. "I'm Blair Kennedy, the station manager. I'm happy to address any concerns you may have, Officer..."

"McBride."

"I see you've met our *new intern*."

She emphasizes the words new and intern like I'm some kind of idiot—which I may be for taking this job.

"Ms. Budewitz told our dispatcher that Ms. McMahon was poisoned."

Blair shakes her head. "I'm sure Ms. Budewitz said Kat was *pale*."

What? I blink. *Poison and pale sound nothing alike.* I glance at Kat, then Wally, and finally back at Blair. Suddenly, I feel like I'm in the middle of a game, and I don't know the rules.

"Isn't that right, Mindy?" Blair nods at me in that encouraging way.

My stomach tightens. My palms sweat. I shift my feet.

Gawkers.

Blair.

Gawkers.

They all continue to stare. The pressure is too much, and I nod *yes*. Even though my mind is screaming *no.*

"Now, that's settled." Blair puts her arm around Blue Bloods' shoulder, her long acrylic nails like talons. "We like to keep incidents like these in house."

Incidents. Has something like this happened before?

"Kat's brand, the station's reputation is everything," Blair continues. "I hope we can count on your discretion." Blair walks Blue Bloods to the exit not waiting for him to respond. "You must join us for Dog Days at the stadium. The network has box seats for the football game."

He smiles and nods.

Lackey.

I can't believe I thought he was cute. And then I realize, if he's a lackey for going along with Blair, then, I'm a lackey too.

"Mindy."

I rip my eyes away from Blue Bloods.

Kat is summoning me. Her face still looks like a blowfish. "Purse."

Despite her *Finding Nemo* appearance, she must be feeling better. Her monosyllabic demands are back in full force. She tells me the code to her dressing room.

I hurry across the set to a door that connects to Dressing Room Row. I find her space, punch in the code. It's the first time I've been allowed inside Kat's sanctuary. It's cluttered with cat-themed pillows, lamps, and artwork. Even the succulent planter on her desk is shaped like a cat. Her cat-studded Dooney and Bourke is on her desk. I reach for it, knock over a picture. When I reposition it, I see the image of Paul and her hairless cat. Paul's horn-rimmed glasses match Dobby's collar, and this somehow adds to the weirdness of my day.

I want to stop, breathe, process—Kat's poisoning, Wally's warning, Blair—but I don't have time. Not if I want to remain in Kat's good graces.

I rush back to the set.

Kat is on a gurney. The paramedics are wheeling her toward the exit. I put the Dooney by her side. I'm not sure she notices. She's too busy reaching for Paul like she's auditioning for a daytime soap opera. "If I don't make it, I want you to know that I will always love you."

Paul looks conflicted. He takes a step forward, and I think he's actually going to leave with her. But Sabrina grabs his arm, and he stops midstride.

Kat's face hardens. "That woman poisoned me. She wants you all to herself, Paul. You can't let her get away with this." The paramedics negotiate the gurney through the door. "She knows I'm allergic to almon—" The door clangs closed.

Almonds. It doesn't take a genius to fill in the blank.

Maybe it wasn't amaretto I smelled when I found Kat. Maybe it was almond milk. The smell could be similar, especially the way Kat sweetens her coffee. There's one way to know for sure. I look for her travel mug. But it's gone—the mug, the spilled coffee. The floor is clean, like nothing ever happened.

I look for Wally.

He's gone, too.

* * * *

I offer to follow Kat to the hospital, but Blair makes me stay. Kat's Korner is supposed to air soon, and she wants me to prep Kat's replacement.

Canine Cal is angling for the job. He makes some corny pitch about how cats and dogs can work together. He smiles at Blair in that used-car-salesmen kind of way.

And she buys it hook, line, and pooch.

"Remember, Cal, we are selling cat products. The demographic is women, fifty-five to sixty-five years old. We need content that resonates, entertains, and educates," Blair says. "Mindy will help you prepare."

Cal tells me to meet him in his dressing room.

I walk through the plastic sheets, past the remodel work and Sabrina's coffee cart, to my cubicle—the one I share with three other interns.

I find my notebook, reorganize the product cards, and grab product manuals in case Cal has specific questions about their features. A few minutes later, I'm standing in front of his dressing room. The door is cracked. I start to knock. But stop short when I hear him on the phone.

"That's right. I'm taking over Kat's Korner."

What? I frown. That's not how Blair pitched it.

"Ten million viewers," he continues. "Crazy right? It's perfect for my demo reel. With this kind of exposure, they have to hire me at SGN."

SGN? It takes me a second to decipher the acronym. Cal is looking for a job at the Sporting Goods Network? I wonder how badly he wants it—enough to spike Kat's coffee and hijack her segment? *Maybe Kat got it wrong. Maybe it wasn't Sabrina who did it.*

My mind is still spinning, when the door flies open.

I scream.

"That's twice in one day, Budewitz."

"Sorry." I'm still breathless. "You startled me."

He folds his arms. "How long have you been standing there?" The tone in his voice is playful. But his eyes, the way they narrow, I can tell he really wants to know if I've overheard his call.

"Not long." I know the answer is vague. I suck at lying. But he seems to accept it because he opens the door wider, and I wonder if I'm about to be alone with a criminal.

I clutch the manuals to my chest like body armor and step inside.

Helmets and footballs fill a bookcase. Large plexiglass frames showcase pictures of Cal on the football field. A dry-erase board with fantasy football draft picks hangs there, too. Which makes sense since Cal is running the fantasy pool for the office. I turn my back to the board, place my things on a table.

"Ready to review the product cards?" I want to get this over with as quickly as possible.

He waves the cards away. "Personal stories, connecting with people. That's what this show needs. Not statistics or product descriptions."

I don't think Blair would agree.

There is a knock at the door. It's his assistant. She tells him it's time to go to hair and makeup.

"Thanks, Mindy," Cal says, dismissing me.

My stomach tightens.

If he tanks the segment, will Blair blame me? What about Kat?

I can nearly hear the tinkling of the ivories, the opening notes of "Let it Go." And I see myself in that godawful costume in a room packed with preschoolers—right before Cal hands me my things and ushers me out the door.

* * * *

"How could you let this happen?" Kat says.

I'm standing in her hospital room. They're keeping her overnight for observation. She's looking better. I can actually look at her face without cringing.

She grabs the remote tethered to her bed and turns up the volume. Cal's voice fills the room. He's sitting in the Glamour-Puss chair talking about how it's the perfect place to watch Monday night football. She groans. "My viewers want to hear about crafting, mystery novels, tea, and above all *cats*."

"He wouldn't let me prep him," I explain while trying to decide if this is a good time to tell her about Cal's quest for that SGN job. I start to speak, but then a hospital volunteer walks in with a bouquet of flowers.

Kat squeals.

I take the flowers and place them on her overbed table. I try not to touch anything else. I have a thing about hospital germs.

"I bet they're from Paul." Kat pushes up in bed, grinning. "It would be just like him to send flowers." She pulls the card from the arrangement. "Get well soon. Love your Pet Shopping Network family."

I smile. "That's nice."

She rips the card in half.

Or not...

She tosses the card aside and folds into a fetal position. "The break-up with Paul. These hives. It's all Sabrina's fault. If Blair had fired her like I'd asked, none of this would've happened."

I shift my feet, not sure what to do. Part of me still wants to tell her about Cal, that Sabrina may not be the enemy. But I know this isn't the time. "What can I do to help?"

"Get me justice, Mindy."

I don't have the guts to tell her that I lied to the police. That the evidence is gone, whisked away by Wally.

That there is no investigation.

She starts crying.

Guilt needles me. Someone needs to stand-up for her. If the police aren't going to investigate, I'm going to have to do it myself.

* * * *

After I bathe my arms in hand sanitizer, I drive back to the studio and make a list of suspects. Despite Cal's revelation, Sabrina's still at the top. Especially now that I know Kat tried to get her fired. Cal, of course, is still a possibility. Then there's Wally—his odd behavior when the police arrived—I wonder if I should look into him, too.

I decide to follow the coffee.

I trek through the remodel and find Sabrina working at the cart. She looks less like a barista and more like an eco-hiker in her thermal shirt and Carhartt overalls. She pours a large drip and hands it to a customer. I wait for him to pay as the line stacks up behind me. Some people are looking for a mid-afternoon caffeine fix. Others are just coming on shift. When it's my turn at the register, I order the most complicated latte on the menu hoping I can steal five minutes of Sabrina's time.

She tugs out a brown paper cup with a green recycle logo. She writes my order on the side, repeats it back to me. I confirm, and she gets to work.

"Well, this has been quite a day," I start.

"That's an understatement." Sabrina scoops espresso into the portafilter, loads it into the machine, presses a button, and the machine hums.

"Are you okay?"

"Why wouldn't I be?"

"It's just Kat—that accusation."

Sabrina shrugs. "Everyone knows she's crazy."

"Crazy for Paul."

Sabrina rolls her eyes. "They've been on and off again for months. Ever since Paul and I started carpooling together, she blames me for their latest breakup."

"So, you're *not* dating?"

She laughs and shakes her head. "I learned a long time ago that dating at work never ends well. Besides Paul isn't my type." The machine clicks off. She pours the espresso into the cup and starts steaming the milk.

"And the almond milk in Kat's coffee?"

"The woman is an Epi-pen waiting to happen. I would never make that mistake." She shows me a laminated sheet lying next to the espresso machine. It has pictures of the on-air talent, their preferences, their food allergies. The list for Kat takes up a quarter of the page. "When Kat ordered her coffee this morning, I pulled a cup, marked it and confirmed it with her just like I did yours. I've been doing it that way since the remodel. Sure, it takes a little longer. But it gets loud, and it helps prevent mistakes."

The noise picks up again. "See what I mean?" Sabrina yells over the hammering.

I nod, half listening, my focus on my phone. I swipe through the pictures until I find the one with the spilled coffee and the travel mug on the floor.

I show the picture to Sabrina. "Did you fill this for Kat?"

She shakes her head. "The woman never brings her own cup to the cart. I'd love if she'd recycle. But from what I've seen, Kat doesn't do anything unless it directly benefits her." Sabrina finishes with the milk, adds it to my cup, dusts it with chocolate. "Kat did the same thing to Wally, accused him of something that he didn't do."

"That's awful."

"She claimed Wally stole a necklace from her dressing room, called the police, and tried to get him fired. Then, like some damsel in distress, she ran to

Paul for help." Sabrina rolls her eyes. "Of course, he helped. He *always* helps. He found the necklace in her office behind one of those ridiculous pillows."

So that's why Wally encouraged me to be quiet when I was questioned by the police. *It had nothing to do with the NDA.* He didn't want someone else falsely accused.

My mind goes to Kat's dramatic exit from the building earlier today. How she reached for Paul. "This thing with Wally, you said Kat ran to Paul. Were they still dating at the time?"

Sabrina frowns, seems to consider, then shakes her head. "I think this was after one of their breakups. But I can't be sure. They're always on again, off again. Sometimes, I think it's their twisted version of foreplay. I hope Paul wakes up and breaks the cycle this time. He deserves better."

I pay Sabrina. "Well, something in that mug made Kat sick."

"Nothing that came from me."

* * * *

I find Wally in the cafeteria, with his plastic tilt truck, doing his daily trash run. I sit at a table, drink my coffee, and wait for him to work his way over to me.

"Hey, Wally."

He's wearing headphones and doesn't seem to hear me. I wave.

He tugs out an earbud. "Afternoon, Mindy."

"Thanks for the heads-up today."

He frowns. "Don't know what you mean."

"On the set, with the police."

He takes the lid off a can, yanks out the bag. The way he's moving, I'm worried if I don't get to the point, he's going to walk away. So, I cut right to it. "I heard Kat accused you of stealing. That she tried to have you fired."

Wally's eyes go wide. "I don't like to dwell on the past." But the way the muscle in his jaw flickers, I know what happened with Kat still bothers him.

I try again, hoping he'll open up to me. "Awful that Kat would jump to a conclusion like that."

"Awful but typical."

"Typical, how?"

"Let's just say, it's nice to see the woman finally got what she deserved."

* * * *

Turns out Wally is less Kris Kringle and more Hells Angels. Unsettled, I walk back to my office. It's packed with interns preparing product cards for tomorrow. I finally snag a computer and half-heartedly respond to emails. My mind is still on the investigation.

My gut tells me Sabrina didn't do it. Which leaves me with Cal and Wally. Both have motive. The question is whether or not they had opportunity.

My phone buzzes.

It's a text from Kat: *Feed Dobby. Key to apartment in desk.*

I leave the computer and head to Dressing Room Row. When I walk past Cal's door, I think about the conversation I overhead this morning—how he wanted Kat's time slot to pad his resumé. It would've been easy for him to slip across the hall, sneak into Kat's room while she was in hair and makeup, and spike her coffee.

If he had the code to her door.

I punch in Kat's code, walk inside, yank out her cluttered desk drawer, grope around for the key, fish out an Epi-Pen instead. I wonder why Kat didn't tell me it was here. Jabbing someone with a needle grosses me out, but I still would've helped her. It takes me another minute, but I finally find the key.

My phone buzzes. Kat again: *Did you find it? Where are you?*

I walk to the door while I text her back and nearly trip over her trashcan. I reach down, rub my shin, and that's when I see it—a cup from Sabrina's cart.

At least it looks like one. It's brown and has the same recycle logo. I wrinkle my nose and fish it out. There's an order on the side in Sabrina's handwriting: half-caf, soy double-shot latte, extra sweet. It's weighty. The cup is still full.

I pull the lid. Inhale.

Nothing that smells like almond milk.

Nothing curdled. It must be from this morning. I'm happy that my instinct about Sabrina was right. Still, I don't understand why Kat would throw out a perfectly good cup of coffee. And why the travel mug?

My phone buzzes.

Another text about Dobby.

I open the door, start to respond, and nearly scream for a third time today.

Wally is standing there with his tilt truck.

Heart jackhammering, I stare at the Ride or Die tattoo on his left triceps and decide my Hells Angels assumption may not be wrong. His back remains toward me, and he's humming along to his music. I dart behind Kat's door, peer outside and wait for him to leave.

He pulls out a universal keycard, bypasses the punch pad, walks into a room. And then it hits me. *Wally has access to the dressing rooms.*

I can't believe I didn't think of this before.

He empties a trash can, continues to Cal's, swipes the lock. Inside, Cal is at the dry-erase board wiping it down.

"Wally!" Cal yells like he's greeting someone on the football field. He claps Wally's shoulder and shakes his hand. "Nicely done, my friend."

Wally nods.

"Really. I'm impressed." Cal reaches into his pocket, pulls out an envelope and hands it to him. "You planned it perfectly."

"Appreciate it, man." Wally opens the envelope. There's cash inside.

My eyes go wide, and I finally connect the dots.

I haven't been looking for one person. I've been looking for two.

Cal paid Wally to poison Kat.

When Wally was cleaning, he saw Sabrina's laminated sheet next to her coffee cart and learned about Kat's almond allergy. He's the one who accessed her dressing room and spiked her coffee. His warning about the cops had nothing to do with protecting Sabrina and everything to do with protecting himself.

I need to tell Blair and force her to do the right thing.

And if that doesn't work, I need to go to the police myself.

* * * *

Blair isn't in her office. Her secretary tells me she went to the hospital to visit Kat. I head to my car to join her there when my phone rings.

It's Kat.

"I have news," I say, excited to tell her what I've learned.

"Dobby, Mindy."

"But—"

"The neighbors. They're apoplectic."

She tells me that Dobby turned up the stereo in her apartment—that he does this when he's hungry, that the neighbors are threatening to call the police.

It seems Dobby is as high-maintenance as his owner.

"Don't bother with kibble, Mindy. *Tuna.* It's the only thing that soothes him. You'll find it in the fridge."

"I'm on it." I open the door to my Ford Fiesta. "I know who spiked your coffee, Kat. It wasn't Sabrina."

She squeals.

I'm glad she's pleased. "I think we need to tell Blair."

I wait for her to respond, to get her blessing. But there's only silence.

"Kat?"

I look at the screen. We're no longer connected. I call her back. It goes to voicemail.

I sigh. It looks like justice will have to wait.

* * * *

When I reach Kat's apartment, Beyoncé is thrumming through the door. I slide the key into the lock and fight the urge to cover my ears while I try to find the source of the noise.

It's the *un-furr-getable* Hello Kitty supersonic sound dock from Monday's show. Dobby is sitting next to the dock on the kitchen counter cleaning his paw. I turn off the music. He paws it on again. I reach over, unplug it, and half expect the cat to plug it back in. It would be a fitting addition to the bizarre list of things that happened today. But Dobby jumps off the counter and saunters away, ending the standoff.

I continue into the kitchen, pull down a bowl, and open the refrigerator. I check the narrow shelves, the doors, any logical place where a small container of tuna may be.

No luck.

I start tugging out cartons of juice, bottles of seltzer. And then I see it—sitting next to the Minute Maid. I stare, dumbfounded.

I was wrong.

I think about the clues I missed: the Epi-Pen, the coffee cup, Kat's history. Her poisoning had nothing to do with Wally or Cal or Sabrina.

It had everything to do with Paul.

* * * *

When I arrive at the hospital, Blair is standing outside Kat's room typing something on her phone. The door is open. Paul is sitting on Kat's bed, arm wrapped around her.

"You knew about the almond milk, didn't you?" I say to Blair, keeping my voice low. "That's why you redirected the police."

Blair nods. "Kat and Paul break up, get back together, break up. They've been doing this for years, and Kat always finds a way to manipulate Paul so he comes back. But this time, putting almond milk in her coffee—making herself sick—it was over the top. Even for her."

I think about the day I've had running around trying to get justice for a woman who did this to herself. I can't decide if I'm angry or if I feel sorry for her. "How can you let things go on like this?"

"I have to balance protecting my people, the station's reputation and keeping Kat happy. She sells more products than any other host. We're all employed because of her."

"You know I thought it was Cal and Wally. That they'd teamed up together." I tell her about the envelope, the cash.

"Fantasy football," Blair explains. "Wally won."

I figured as much.

"Mindy," Kat waves.

I look at Blair, not sure what to do, but her face is back in her phone. So, I take a deep breath and proceed inside.

Kat is practically beaming. "How's Dobby?"

"Fed," I say, fighting to keep my voice neutral.

"Thank you."

I think this is the first polite thing she's ever said to me.

She snuggles closer to Paul. "There's something you wanted to tell me?"

Every fiber of my being wants to dime her out. To tell Paul that he's been suckered again. But on some level, I think Blair is right. He already knows. "It's nothing."

"I appreciate all your help today, Mindy. I spoke to Blair. It's official." She clasps her hands together like a giddy schoolgirl. "No more interning. I want you to be my full-time assistant."

"Welcome to the Pet Shopping Network family," Paul says.

A dysfunctional one.

I think about Sabrina, about Wally. Who knows, next month I may be the one in Kat's crosshairs. Suddenly, my mother's princess party business doesn't seem so bad after all. At least kids are predictable.

When I pull away from the hospital, I can hear the tinkling of the ivories, the opening notes of "Let it Go," and for the first time I'm happy to go home.

Stacy Woodson (stacywoodson.com) made her crime fiction debut in *Ellery Queen's Mystery Magazine*'s Department of First Stories and won the 2018 Readers Award. Since her debut, she has placed stories in several anthologies and publications—two winning the Derringer award.

AN UNPOPULAR GALLERY

DARREN GOOSSENS

Shoulders drooping, Steve walked into the quiet of the Nineteenth Century Collection. The familiar array of paintings in their heavy gilt frames, and the emptiness of the room, encouraged him to relax a little. He saw Charlie Earp's broad, round back in front of the Manet at the far end of the discreetly lit gallery. Steve's booted footsteps and the click of his badge against its belt clip allowed Charlie to raise a hand in greeting without turning around. The same hand gestured at the free space on the bench.

Steve sat down with a nasal grunt. He put his hands on his knees and let his head fall forward.

"I hate Tuesdays," he said.

He stared at the polished boards.

"Didn't know you were Greek," said Charlie through his silver beard.

Steve sat up and looked at Charlie Earp, Greenvale Fine Art Gallery's most regular regular. He visited far more often than the mediocre collection warranted. Usually he just looked at the Manet, the only really world-class piece in the place.

Steve sighed. "Don't care about Greeks right now, Professor. Aztecs, yes. Aztec gold, even more. Especially an Aztec snake stick thing that went missing this morning."

Charlie did not take his eyes off the painting. He always told Steve it was the girl's eyes he found so fascinating, but Steve wondered if it was some other part of her anatomy.

"Constantinople fell on a Tuesday," said Charlie.

"And chances are Peta Davidson is going to fire me on a Tuesday." Peta Davidson was the new Director of the Greenvale Gallery. She held big ideas about "capitalizing on emerging media" and "recasting our mission in terms of a broader social agenda." Whatever that meant.

At last Charlie turned to face the security guard. "Going to get sacked by a young Turk yourself, eh?"

Steve muttered, unsure of the reference.

"Couldn't help myself," Charlie said, "What's happened?"

"You know the exhibition of Aztec art we're hosting at the moment? The one that the Director fought like hell to bring to Greenvale?"

"'Greenvale Fine Art Gallery is proud to be the only regional venue to host the exhibition,'" Charlie quoted.

"Yeah. That one. Well. Most of it is clay, feathers, and rocks as far as I can see. But there are half a dozen golden pieces. Some earrings, a medallion, even a lip pin, I think they call it, that you wear through a slit in your lip." He made a face. "And, until this morning, a sort of long thin rod, maybe a foot long, with a snake's head and a pointy tail. Bit like a knitting needle with a face."

"And it's been lost?"

"Stolen, and I think I know who, but he didn't have it on him when…" Steve shrugged. "I don't know. Maybe Peta's right. Maybe it's time I went." He shifted his weight back and forth on the lacquered wooden seat.

Charlie, old, overweight, and of necessity skilled in the art of sitting still, merely clucked. "Who is 'he'?"

"Paul Simpson, if his ID is real. Tall, thin, wears a big coat. Well, he did this morning."

"Gray coat? Lots of pockets?"

Steve sat up a little. "You know him?"

"Not at all, but I've seen him in here before." Charlie squeezed his lower lip, his eyes drifting back to Manet's young lady.

"Probably casing the joint."

"But he didn't have it?"

"He didn't have anything on him except his wallet and a wristwatch—not even a phone. He was looking in all the display cases in the exhibition gallery, and I just got that feeling that he was… I just got suspicious, can't say why for sure. Years in the job, I guess. I was in the chair near the entry to this gallery, and the case with the gold rod was up the other end of the room. He finished looking and started wandering toward Home Furnishings—"

"You mean 'Decorative Arts,'" chuckled Charlie.

"Yeah, the room where nobody goes. I got up and started to walk after him, not rushing or anything. I looked around as I went, and noticed that the thing was missing. I radioed the front desk to close off the Gallery and kept after the guy. It was a typical weekday—I had to edge around two grannies, an old man in a wheelchair and some kids from a school group, but soon I was in Home Furnishings. Took me maybe half a minute. Nobody else was there but me and him. It's a dead-end room. I asked him to come to the foyer. I said we'd had a possible theft and we were clearing the gallery, checking people out one by one. It's in the conditions of entry, all that stuff."

Charlie tilted his head. He spoke softly. "And he didn't complain?"

Steve shook his head. "Nope, just walked out with me, almost too casual. We ran the metal detector over him, took his name and address, and let him out. Did the same with everybody else—even inspected the wheelchair. Boy was that guy grumpy. Lucky it was still early and not many people were in yet. We spent the next five hours turning the place upside down, and only reopened about half an hour ago."

"What have you told the public?"

"Peta put a card in the case. It says, 'this exhibit is undergoing restoration.'" Steve snorted. "Restoration to its proper owners, I hope."

"How did he get it out of the case?"

"Come and have a look."

Steve braced his hands on his knees and began to push himself up. Charlie patted his rotund belly, hooked a thumb behind one of his braces, and remained unmoved.

"Later," he said. "Just tell me. My knees are giving me hell."

That was true enough, Steve knew. Charlie walked with a knock-kneed gait, a compromise between his sense of dignity and his overloaded joints.

"Well, I found a hole in the glass sidewall of the case, just big enough to put your hand through. It must have been cut with some kind of diamond tool."

"But he didn't have the cutter on him, and you didn't find it anywhere?"

"No. There was transparent tape on the circle of glass. He even put it back after he took the piece. Must have cut it out some other day, probably working underneath that coat. The security camera footage from this morning shows him just leaning on the case. Can't see anything, and he's not even the only person who's ever leaned against it—kids do it all the time to get a better look—but I bet if we go back through the records we'll find him leaning on it some other time, before."

Charlie nodded appreciatively. "And then you searched everywhere."

Steve nodded emphatically. "We turned the whole place upside down, but especially Home Furnishings. We checked the vases, even the Chinese one, all those eighteenth century fancy tables and chairs. We even squashed all the cushions in case he'd cut a slit in one and poked it in there. At least Peta stopped hassling me while we were in there—I told her just last week that we needed to install cameras in *all* the galleries. I mean, there's no room in the budget, but me and Vladislav, we can't be everywhere. She said at the time," Steve pursed his lips and spoke in a strangulated, vaguely female voice, "'And tell me precisely *who* is going to hide a George III carved mahogany Chippendale silver *table* under their jacket?' I told her we needed more cameras. She just thought I wanted to skive off or something. Are you listening?" He leaned forward and tried to catch Charlie's attention.

Charlie brought his eyes back into focus and looked away from the Manet. "The clock?"

Steve smiled with some affection. "Yes, Charlie, we even searched your clock."

"I just admire it. It's a beautiful piece of engineering. Recoil escapement, two-second pendulum with a lightweight pendulum rod. Coarse and fine adjustments. Keeps better than a minute a week." He looked at Steve. "I guess I'm still an engineer at heart."

"Well, we searched it. We looked in the case, even though it needs a key. We checked to see if he'd taped the snake onto the back of it, sat it on top, shoved it underneath, we even looked to see if he'd stuck it to the back of the pendulum. You name it."

Charlie chewed his mustache in thought. "He didn't 'hide' it in its own case?"

"No."

"You checked the cushions, but what about the room itself? On top of doorframes, window sashes, that sort of thing?"

A hint of impatience passed like the thinnest of clouds across Steve's face. "Yes, Charlie."

"Air vents?"

"We looked, Charlie. We checked the light fittings even though they're eight feet off the floor. We checked the rafters in case he'd tossed it up there."

"No holes in the windows, where he might have passed it out?"

"For Chrissakes, Charlie. We even screwed off the light switches in case he'd shoved it into the wall cavity, though he didn't have a screwdriver on him."

Charlie waggled a finger at the ceiling. Steve imagined the old man tottering back and forth in front of a class of undergraduates, pontificating on some obscure point of metallurgy or mechanical engineering.

Charlie said, "He could have come in with all sorts of things. He could have made a box, stained it to match the existing wood, put the golden snake in the box and stuck it to one of the bits of furniture. Do any of your bits of furniture have a new component?"

Steve opened his mouth to say: "No, Charlie," then realized he was not so sure. He said: "He had no glue on him."

"He can put that in the box before he sticks it into place. Could be a long thin box that looks like a bit of dowel or edging. When it all dies down he comes back, knocks it loose and walks out."

Charlie sat back and folded his arms.

"He'll never get back in without being watched. I'll guarantee you that. But I'll suggest one of the curators examine the furniture with extra woodwork in mind." Steve stood up. "Well, thanks, Professor. I better go see if I'm still in the bad books. Vladislav will be wanting some help in the exhibition gallery, and then I'll have to start looking for work."

"Surely she won't really fire you."

"Tell you the truth, I'm not sure."

Charlie shook his head in sympathy and opened his mouth to speak, then closed it again.

They listened with half-smiles as the warm bell-tones of the clock chimed out three p.m., a faint sound two rooms away. Out of habit Charlie looked down at his wrist. He frowned.

"What?" Steve crouched. "Charlie, are you OK?"

"It's not angina, Steve. Have you got the time?"

"It's three. We just—"

"On your watch. Exactly."

Steve pulled his phone out of his jacket pocket. "OK, two fifty-nine."

Charlie smiled in triumph. "I know where your golden snake is."

Steve's eyes widened, then began to roll. He caught himself and held out a hand. He hauled Charlie to his feet and they went out into the exhibition gallery, Charlie refusing to explain.

In the Decorative Arts gallery, Charlie stomped toward the clock. Steve radioed the front desk, and after considerable cajoling the receptionist agreed to ask for someone to bring them the key for the clock case.

It was Peta Davidson, thin lipped, grim, and more than a little harassed. Charlie asked to inspect the key. She thrust it at him as if it were a knife and he a mugger. He plucked it from her grip with the look of a man defusing a bomb. It proved to be very simple and generic, and no doubt anyone with even a little skill at lock-picking could have opened the door. Or simply obtained an equivalent key.

Inspecting Charlie but speaking to Steve, she said: "Please let's get this over with. You have no idea how busy I am right now. You have no idea how difficult it was to get this exhibition into a small gallery out in the sticks. This will ruin our reputation, ruin *my* reputation. If this situation were not so desperate…"

Charlie laid his handkerchief on his left hand and with his right swung open the door to reveal the pendulum. He reached down to the bottom of the bob, grabbed the adjustment nut and yanked it down.

Several things happened.

The pendulum bob slapped into Charlie's waiting left hand.

Peta Davidson's face went white.

The golden snake fell out of the hollow pendulum rod and clattered against the base of the case.

Steve whooped for joy.

Charlie held out the snake of golden wire. Peta took it.

"For this clock to gain a minute in four or five hours, the pendulum had to be appreciably shortened. This snake is around a foot long, much longer than the diameter of a pendulum bob. Poking it up into the hollow pendulum rod moves the center of mass of the pendulum up, and speeds it up. And I knew it was hollow because of its close-to-ideal, lightweight design."

Peta gaped, a smile more of relief than pleasure slowly softening her face. Steve merely grinned and slapped Charlie on the back.

Charlie was clearly fighting to keep a look of smugness off his face. "I guessed that our thief, who clearly prepared ahead, might also have modified the pendulum for a 'quick release' of the threaded stub that holds the adjustment nuts. He would have had time. This is not a popular gallery."

Over her shoulder Peta's eyes said thank you, but her legs were already carrying her back to the exhibition gallery, where a glazier had repaired the violated display case.

"Fantastic," said Steve. "I owe you a couple of beers. Charlie, we searched the guy—he didn't have any tool to open the case."

Charlie held up the very simple key. "A plastic copy of a key from a similar clock would do the job, I dare say."

They left the pendulum, and any fingerprints it might bear, sitting on Charlie's handkerchief on the floor of the clock case, then locked up the clock. As they left the room, Steve, relief coursing through him, found it difficult to walk as slowly as Charlie.

Steve said: "Don't worry, we'll post a watch for that guy. When he comes back, we'll be waiting."

"He won't come back, and I would be shocked if his ID was real. But, would you recognize the man in the wheelchair if he walked in?"

"You're a wise man, Professor."

Charlie beamed. "You might be right."

Darren Goossens is a writer and editor, and former physicist, based near Canberra, Australia. He has published a few stories over the years, but this is his first mystery.

BOOK LEARNING

K.L. ABRAHAMSON

The air was full of spring softness and sunlight and the scent of newly turned earth from the flower gardens surrounding the cottages of Sandcastle Lane as Betty-Lynn Merchant shuffled down her driveway in her shin-length, pink floral caftan and her fluffy pink slippers.

The Lane, as everyone who lived there called it, was a one-block-long strip of the old-fashioned, ivy-strewn, small, one-story cottages that once had been all that existed in Davis Bay. Now, aside from the Lane, most of the cottages were gone, replaced with glass, wood, and Hardie Board-clad homes, some of which topped three stories.

But the Lane remained, as did the old-timers who lived there, much to the old timers' satisfaction. They kept to themselves, grew prodigious gardens, held an annual garden party—or two—and enjoyed their book club. Most of all they enjoyed their books. Many was the time neighbors could be found leaning on their fences, discussing the latest Debbie Macomber or Clive Cussler. Better than a water cooler for exchanging news was the tiny community library that stood outside Betty-Lynn's house.

Her dearly departed Howard had built the miniature house on a post. But what had started as a planned bread-box-sized place to drop off books for Betty-Lynn, the acknowledged fastest reader in the Lane, had, under Howard's careful hands and prodigious imagination, become a tiny ornate gabled cottage complete with scalloped gray siding and white trim that matched the Merchant house. The glass door on the little library was always unlocked to allow anyone to access the books inside. A small brass plaque read "Please enjoy your reading. Take a book. Leave one behind."

Betty-Lynn stopped at the corner of her driveway and Sandcastle Lane. Before she could open the library door, a man lying at the base of her cedar hedge caught her attention.

She cleared her throat. The man didn't move.

From beyond the white picket fence that framed Tanzy Henry's front yard came the snuffling of Rufus, her white terrier.

"Excuse me. You can't sleep there. There's a shelter in town if you need one."

Still no response. There was only the twittering of birds and the soft sigh of the ocean wind in the trees.

Hesitantly, she stepped across the damp grass, dreading the mess the dew was going to make of her fluffy slippers. She bent down and jiggled his shoulder. His face flopped toward her, his eyes milky and his red mouth wide.

That was when she recognized Trevor McNally. That was when she screamed.

And that was where I came in.

I've lived across from Betty-Lynn these past thirty-odd years. We've read romance together. We've read women's fiction. We went through a fantasy stage and agreed that Tolkien's saga far outstripped any of his emulators. Lately our tastes had diverged, with Betty-Lynn putting on airs because she was reading literary fiction, while I had dived deep into mysteries. But for all her airs, she was still a simple woman who liked to place garden gnomes beneath her trees and hedges.

So, of course, when I heard the scream, I had to investigate.

Betty-Lynn's thin white legs marched in place like she was stuck in neutral, her favorite pink slippers sodden from the grass, her eyes almost as wide as the dead man's. I recognized Trevor's ragged, gray hair. He wore the same red plaid shirt and baggy jeans I'd seen him wear in his garden the previous day. What I didn't recognize was the blood on his forehead and the dent in his head. He was most certainly dead.

I took a deep breath and caught Betty-Lynn's hand. This was what I'd waited my whole life for. A crime in my own backyard. "Stop," I said. "Stop screaming. He's dead is all."

Betty-Lynn turned her wild gaze to me, and she threw herself into my arms. "Oh my God. Oh my God. What are we going to do, Clara?"

I held her away from me. We were friends, but I'd always found Betty-Lynn's damsel-in-distress act a little off-putting and more so since her Howard died. Trevor and I seemed to be the ones she always turned to for rescuing. "We call the police, of course, and stop you from wrecking the scene any more than you already have."

I eased her away from the body but studied the damp grass as I went. Betty-Lynn's trail was evident, but there was another, fainter one that led along the cedars, past a straggling line of garden gnomes, to Trevor's driveway, as if whoever had killed Trevor had walked away in that direction. Of course, it could just be Trevor's path, and Betty-Lynn could have obliterated the killer's footsteps.

Holding her arm, I led her up the driveway and inside. The little gray-sided cottage was cheerful inside and out. Outside, Betty-Lynn's crocuses and hellebores were in bloom in the shadow of her red-barked arbutus tree. Inside, two chairs and an overstuffed couch covered with pristine white slipcovers were precisely arranged over oriental rugs and gleaming hardwood floors. Family photos decorated the walls and most flat surfaces.

I set her to making herself a cup of tea. Then I phoned 911 and followed that up with a call to Mavis so someone could sit with Betty-Lynn while I waited for the police and protected the scene.

Mavis arrived within five minutes, tsk-tsking at the situation. She was a thin woman, with gray hair dyed ridiculously black. Today it was damp and coiffed like a helmet. Her abhorrence of creases meant she had a penchant for polyester pull-on trousers and pressed-within-an-inch-of-their-lives T-shirts. Today her trousers were red.

"A body!" Mavis said as she made her usual slight pause at the door. "Who would have believed it? And right out there on the lawn where anyone could see! And on Sandcastle Lane! Simply unacceptable! Who do you think could have done such a thing?" Mavis liked to think she could set the standard for behavior on Sandcastle Lane. She was the first one complaining and taking action if one of us changed the color of our house or removed a large shrub from our gardens. Not much of one for change, our Mavis.

The ambulance showed up before I got outside. The police showed up about ten minutes later, after I'd left Betty-Lynn and Mavis discussing who Trevor's next of kin might be and what they might do with the cottage they'd likely be inheriting. It was a troubling thought given any sale of a cottage in the area seemed to lead to the construction of one of those behemoth houses. Something like that would destroy Sandcastle Lane.

The first two police officers were a couple of young constables who taped off the area. They asked my name and whether I knew the dead man.

"Trevor McNally. He lives—excuse me—lived right there." I pointed out the yellow clapboard cottage with the peaked roof you could just see over the hedges between Trevor and Betty-Lynn's properties. "He's lived here about fifteen years. Moved out from the city. A newcomer to the area. He hasn't quite fit in yet." I shook my head. The fact was that Trevor had never fully fit in and now never would.

"Is he single? Married? Who were his friends?"

"He's single. A widower. Friends? I suppose we are—his neighbors and all. I never saw him with other people."

A sleek gray SUV pulled up and another man climbed out. He conferred with one of the uniformed police and then came to me. He was young—maybe about forty—with squint lines around his no-nonsense brown gaze. He had coarse, sandy brown hair that looked like it hadn't seen a comb in years, and he wore khaki trousers and a blue windbreaker, like he was a tourist. Good God, another newcomer.

"Sergeant Mark Thiessen. And you are?"

"Clara Smythe. I live across the street." I motioned to my pristine white cottage, the prettiest on the street, in my opinion. I've always had a way with gardens and my pink azaleas were, as usual, the first to bloom profusely.

"You found the body?"

"Um. No." I told him about Betty-Lynn. "I kept her from traipsing all over your scene and took her up to the house. She's having tea with Mavis at the moment."

"Mavis?"

"Our neighbor two doors down that way. I thought Betty-Lynn would do better with company." I glanced over to where the paramedics had packed up and a new group of technicians were examining the body. They'd come in their own van while I was talking to the Sergeant. "So, who do you think killed him?"

He raised his head from taking notes. "Maybe you can tell me more about Trevor McNally, first. I understand you told the other officer that he hasn't fit into the community."

"Well… he's been here fifteen years, so I suppose he's fit in some." I thought a moment. "It's little things, I guess. Painting his house that atrocious yellow when clearly the Lane prefers white, soft blues, and grays. All you have to do is look around." I motioned up and down the street where our lovely cottages gleamed. "He did that a year ago, but that was only the most recent of his transgressions. The worst was when he cut down two cedar trees just after he moved in. We were horrified and people around here have long memories. It felt like he'd murdered two friends, but he said they put too much shade on his yard." I shook my head.

Sergeant Thiessen made a show of considering his notes, but I caught the doubtful glances he threw at me from the tops of his eyes. "So, cutting down the trees made the neighbors mad at him."

"True. But that was years ago. Since then, he's been a pretty good neighbor. At least until he painted his house. He's—he was really good with tools and used to help us out with small jobs that needed doing. A lot of us on Sandcastle Lane have lost our husbands and then there're a few spinsters. Not too many men around anymore since Betty-Lynn lost her Howard. I think Trevor liked showing off his handyman skills. A knight to the rescue, if you will. Some of the ladies adored him."

"Did Trevor have any other friends? Any enemies that you know of?"

I stopped for a moment, thinking and scanning the crowd that had gathered. All were my friends. There was Wilma Cornish, who owned the cottage across from Trevor's. She was a wisp of a thing with long blond hair she kept in a twist, who liked to wear flowing caftans. Today she wore an atrocious shade of chartreuse. She had always seemed a little sweet on Trevor. There was Sandra Delmonico, who liked to call herself Sandra Dee. She'd had Trevor over to fix her bathroom caulking too many times for me to count. Another 'friend' of Trevor's?

And then there was Cassy Blake, whose stage name had been Cassandra Blake. She had thinning white hair she wore close to her skull. At the moment her diminutive form was plastered into the hulking side of Herman Hoffsteder. Herman's house stood at the far end of the block and actually had an address on the cross street. Even so, he was considered an honorary resident of the Lane because he kept his small home in the same spirit as the rest of us. He'd also dated most of the ladies at one time or another. But a friend of Trevor's?

Never.

"Not that I know of. There was only us."

The forensics team were allowing the paramedics to remove the body while they examined the lawn around where the body had lain.

"There was a trail in the grass leading back toward Trevor's," I said.

"Pardon me?" Sergeant Thiessen asked, his gaze coming up from his notes. Apparently, he'd lost interest in whatever he'd been writing.

"You can't see it now, because the sun has evaporated the dew, but there was a trail in the grass from Trevor's driveway to his body. Now maybe it was just his own track from when he came this way, but it might also have been how the killer left. Betty-Lynn had already ruined any sign of tracks around the body."

"Interesting." He tapped his pen on his notepad. "There's no sign of a trail, now. You say that's the victim's home there?"

I nodded.

"Why would he be out here early in the morning?"

I shrugged and watched the forensics team examining the grass, marking bits of evidence that I hadn't spotted, and photographing everything before collecting and bagging it. It really was quite as impressive in real life as I'd imagined from my mystery books.

"Ms. Smythe? Clara? I asked why he'd be out here."

"That's easy. The books of course." I motioned to the library. The sun was higher and glared off the grass front. "He liked to get out here early. A number of people in the area like to leave new books in the evening. He liked to have first pick." I shook my head.

"Was that a problem? You don't look happy."

"Well, a number of us read quite quickly so we always look forward to new books. Trevor had a habit of taking all the new titles but being quite slow to finish and return the books. It had become something of a race to see who got to the library first."

"I see," he nodded. "So, Trevor McNally was friends with the lady residents of the block, but annoyed some of them, too."

Obviously. I nodded.

Down the block Rufus was barking at all the commotion in the Lane. Other residents were coming out of their homes to see what the fuss was. Gradually, a crowd was gathering, and the uniformed officers were urging them back from the scene. I have to say I straightened a little straighter at being in the center of things.

"Was Trevor McNally dating anyone? He was single and so were many of the neighbors. Anything happening there?"

I felt a flush of color up my cheeks. Trevor and I had gone out once, but there were no fireworks between us. "Of course, there was dating. A lot of flirting, too."

"Anyone in particular?"

I told him about Wilma Cornish and Sandra Delmonico. "I know he took Dixey—that's Dixey Fernly—out for dinner last week. And he'd had dinner with Betty-Lynn a few times, too, since her Howard passed." I shrugged.

"Any animosity between the ladies over Trevor?"

It was a good question that got me thinking because Dixey and Betty-Lynn had never been the best of friends. They more tolerated each other. "I honestly don't know."

"But you could guess." He raised his brows at me, and I was glad the crowd was farther away so they couldn't hear me. I told him what I knew.

"But I can't imagine any of those ladies killing Trevor. It looked like quite a violent crime—hitting someone over the head."

His brows rose a little higher and his jaw worked. "What makes you say that?"

"I saw the body close up, Sergeant. I saw the shape of his head and the blood. That kind of blow comes with anger, and I can't see any of the ladies we've discussed being mad at Trevor. At each other, maybe, though Wilma and Sandra's involvement is all past, so I don't even think they'd be mad. I also doubt any of them have the strength." I paused. "Well, Sandra, maybe. She does keep in shape with her power walking and aquafit."

He eyed me thoughtfully. "You're quite an observant woman."

"I try. I read mysteries. I usually know who did it before the killer is revealed. I've become quite good at it, actually."

"Did you happen to hear or see anything earlier this morning?"

"Not until Betty-Lynn screamed."

His lips curved in a small suppressed smile as if he was humoring me. Typical police reaction to the gifted amateur detective. It was that look that made me determined to solve the crime, though I wasn't quite certain how.

He closed his notebook. "I think that's all my questions for now, except do you happen to know anyone who might be able to comment on the state of Trevor McNally's home? You know, who might notice if something was missing? Perhaps one of the ladies he's been dating?"

"I've been inside a number of times. A few of us—Trevor, Betty-Lynn, Mavis, Tanzy, and I had a bit of a book club going. I—I have his emergency key." Of course, the book club had been on a bit of hiatus lately.

His dark brows rose again as if this was an intimacy that placed me on his suspects list. I really needed to steer him correctly.

"If he had just stepped out to go to the library, I suspect we won't need your key. Why don't you come with me, Ms. Smythe? But first of all, could you take a look in the library and tell me what you see?"

He used a glove to pull open the library's small glass door, releasing the lovely scent of paper, ink, and glue.

I scanned the titles, most of them the familiar tomes that had been around the community too many times. A few that were still making the rounds. No new titles. I told him so and then turned to where Trevor's body had been. There'd been no books under his body, either. When I looked back at the Sergeant, I knew he'd noticed it too.

We headed for Trevor's driveway.

"Was it kids? I'll bet it was kids who did this. Too many of them cutting through the Lane on those damned bikes of theirs," Herman Hoffsteder called.

Sergeant Thiessen slowed his pace, almost as if he was eager for such an obvious suspect. "Have there been problems?"

I shook my head. "It's the kids from the new development on their way to school. They're noisy and not very good at putting their litter in the trash, but I wouldn't see them as suspects."

Trevor's bright-yellow cottage had a deep-blue door with a shiny brass knocker shaped like a buxom mermaid. When Sergeant Thiessen tried the door, it opened, and we stepped into the tiny vestibule that served as Trevor's mudroom. I toed my shoes off as usual, though the Sergeant didn't.

Contrary to Trevor's tidy garden, the inside of his house always reminded me of a recently shaken snow globe.

The living room was a clutter of books stacked helter-skelter on every flat surface. The only clear space was Trevor's preferred lounger next to a small side table, both of which were surrounded by more books. These were opened face down on the table and on the floor.

I must have winced for Sergeant Thiessen pinned me with his eagle eye. "What is it? Is something missing?"

I shook my head. "It's the books, is all. It looks like he's broken all the spines."

Thiessen looked confused.

"May I?" When he nodded, I retrieved one of the books from off the floor. "You see, a book spine is what holds the book together. In paperbacks it's glue. In hardbacks its glue and binding. By leaving a book open face down, or by bending the covers back too far—I cringe when I see people read a paperback with one cover curled back around the back of the book—it wrecks the binding. With paperbacks in particular it can lead to pages falling out. I would never loan a book to someone who breaks a book's spine." I glanced at the book I held. *A Horticulturalist's Diary.* One of the classics.

A small space on the coffee table had been cleared for a fine china plate with an oriental design. It was something Trevor had picked up on his travels and always used to serve snacks when our small book club convened. A single piece of cheese lay forgotten, its edges dried. Beside the plate, two wine glasses sat, one with red lipstick on the rim.

"Mm-hmm," Sergeant Thiessen said. He pulled gloves on. "Please don't touch anything else. This may be part of the crime scene."

Well, sure. It was a crime what had been done to those books. I kept turning back to the books left broken on the floor. The titles were some I remembered as Trevor's pride and joy.

I followed Sergeant Thiessen into the kitchen where the stink of burning coffee permeated the room. It was its usual disarray. Used tea bags on the counter. Unwashed dishes in the sink. A pot simmered in a coffee maker that was still turned on. In the toaster, two slices of bread had popped, but were now cold. On the kitchen table sat two more stacks of books. Beside them was a coffee cup. Trevor's world had always been his garden and his books.

But these books were some I'd been hoping to find in the little library this morning. Tanzy had said she had received them from her son-in-law and would be putting them out once she'd read them. They hadn't been in the library yesterday so she must have put them out last night.

"I don't think the wine glasses have anything to do with Trevor's death. He was alive this morning."

"Agreed," Sergeant Thiessen said.

"May I?" I asked, indicating the books on the table.

He arched a brow "why?" at me.

"I just want to check something."

He studied the room as if seeking some relevance of the books to the murder and finally shrugged. "Go ahead."

I slipped into the seat Trevor must have used and looked at the cup. Many lines of dried coffee suggested that the cup had been drained and refilled a number of times. I scanned the book titles and picked up the book on the top of a pile of three books. I fanned it open and riffled the pages. There was nothing there, except here and there, little folds on page corners. Someone had dog-eared them and then unfolded the corners after they had finished reading. I picked up the top book from the second pile and performed the same action. There were no dog-ears.

I slumped back in Trevor's chair feeling sick to my stomach. "I think… I think know who killed him."

"What? From looking at a pile of books?"

I nodded. "You're forgetting that I know these people, perhaps better than I want to." I stood up and faced the good Sergeant, who looked at me with clear disbelief. "I suggest we bring Tanzy, Betty-Lynn, and Mavis together."

"What about the women who were dating Trevor. You mentioned"—he flipped open his notebook—"this Dixey woman. And Wilma and Sandra."

"We can include them if you like. Perhaps Betty-Lynn will allow us to use her living room to meet."

By the downturn of Sergeant Thiessen's lips, he wasn't convinced I had his answer, but maybe sergeant work was slow that day, or maybe he was looking for a story to tell the other sergeants about a silly old woman who learned her investigation techniques from mystery stories. Either way, he humored me, and we adjourned from Trevor's home out to the street, where I gathered the people I'd named before we retreated to Betty-Lynn's.

Betty-Lynn, having overcome her shock and enjoying the notoriety that came with having discovered the body, bustled around making tea for everyone. Then we all settled on her slip-covered living room furniture with Sergeant Thiessen hovering far too conspicuously in the corner.

"As you know," I began, "our friend and neighbor and book buddy Trevor McNally has been murdered."

There were nods all around, though Sergeant Thiessen rolled his eyes.

"Sergeant Thiessen has kindly agreed to allow this little talk so that hopefully we can solve this horrific event." I looked from person to person. Betty-Lynn clutched her pink caftan tightly at the neck as if afraid of exposing herself, but perhaps she simply couldn't warm up. Mavis sat cool and crisp in her polyester trousers and blouse, her arm around Betty-Lynn's shoulders. Tanzy, a scrawny chicken of a woman with fly-away gray hair who always wore coveralls and a threadbare flannel shirt, perched on the edge of the couch. Beside her sat Dixey, with her sequined top and her neat cap of white hair. On dining room chairs, dragged in for this gathering, sat Wilma and Sandra. All were my friends, but one of them was a murderer. Still, all of them met my gaze so well, I wondered whether I was wrong.

"Wilma and Sandra, you both dated Trevor a number of times. Can you tell us the last time you were with the man?"

Wilma fingered the chartreuse fabric of her caftan. "I spoke to him over the fence yesterday. I offered him coffee and crumb cake, but he said he was busy—just finishing his walk you see." She shook her head sadly. Yes, Wilma still carried a torch for Trevor.

"And you, Sandra?" I asked.

"Well. We weren't dating anymore, if you must know. But he was over a week ago to finish the caulking in my bathroom. For some reason it was developing mold, but it's all fine now," Sandra said with a dare in her gaze as if to challenge anyone who made any inferences.

I thanked her and turned to the couch. "Betty-Lynn. Dixey. You were both dating Trevor, weren't you?"

The two women looked at each other and smiled.

"Trevor was fun," Dixey said. "We'd gone out a few times, but I wouldn't call it dating. Trevor might have been fun, but he was cheap. We always went Dutch on our little excursions."

Betty-Lynn sighed. "I liked Trevor, I really did, but it was too soon for me to think of him as anything other than a friend. Besides, his house was always a mess. I couldn't abide a man like that. It—it would take too long to train him!"

Light laughter made a circuit of the room. Trevor might be fun, but none of us were desperate for a relationship with him. At least not desperate enough to kill him.

I glanced at the good sergeant and saw that he was paying attention.

"Tanzy, you placed seven new books in the library last night. Am I right?"

She nodded, brushing stray stands of hair from her eyes.

"What time did you put them there?" I asked.

"I—I'm not sure, exactly. I—I—It was late. After the late news. I was ready for bed when I finished the last book. I—I could have left them to the morning, but I knew other people wanted them." She smiled at me. Tanzy had a penchant for mysteries, too.

"It must have been close to midnight," she finished. "I took Rufus for a last walk at the same time."

"So, you took the books out there and placed them in the library."

She nodded.

"Did you happen to notice anyone around?"

She shook her head, but then stopped. "Hold on. There was something. I didn't see anyone, but Rufus acted funny. He barked at shadows."

Ah-ha.

"Thank you, Tanzy." I looked around at the ladies present. "I don't know about you, but I've been getting up earlier and earlier trying to be first to get to the new books. So far it hasn't worked, and someone has always cleaned out the new books by the time I get there. I think you've found the same. By the time I get them, the books are usually well-worn with dog-ears and broken spines—something that was a great point of discussion amongst some of us." I looked pointedly at Tanzy, Betty-Lynn, and Mavis, but they wouldn't meet my gaze.

"Ms. Smythe, is this going somewhere? I have an investigation to conduct," Sergeant Thiessen said. He'd closed his notebook and placed it in his pocket, so clearly I'd lost his interest.

Darn it.

I held up a hand to stop his interruption and turned back to Betty-Lynn. "Betty-Lynn, you belonged to the same book club as Mavis, Tanzy, Trevor, and me, correct?"

She nodded, the relief in her gaze saying she appreciated the easy question.

"Has that book club been meeting lately?"

"N—n—no. You know it hasn't."

"Can you tell us why?"

She looked at me pleadingly, but finally sighed. "There was an argument."

"Yes. What was the argument about?"

"How to care for books." Her voice had gotten softer.

"It was a nasty argument," Tanzy chipped in, nodding. "I don't actually get it. A book is to be enjoyed, but it's also a special thing. Something to be cared for so that the stories can be shared. Otherwise, the books fall apart, and no one gets to enjoy them anymore." She glanced at Mavis and looked away.

"Do either of you recall the chief complaints in the argument?"

Betty-Lynn glanced at Mavis and then down at her hands. Tanzy said nothing.

"Oh, for goodness sake," Dixey said, sunlight through the living room window glittering on her sequins. "Even I've heard about the argument. I suspect everyone on the Lane has. Trevor had a bad habit of dog-earing his books. Mavis couldn't abide that habit, but regularly broke the spines of books she read. Trevor might not have been perfect—he did chop down those trees—but he was rabid about protecting book spines."

All eyes in the room turned to Mavis, even those of Sergeant Thiessen. Mavis's arm slipped from Betty-Lynn's shoulders and then she stood. Her fingers smoothed her T-shirt flat over her slight tummy.

"All of you! All of you simpering after that man simply because he *was* a man. Every book he touched, he ruined, dog-earing the pages. He even folded an entire page in half at times, simply to spite me. I knew what he was doing so I started to wait for books to be delivered so that I could get them before him. It became a race between the two of us."

Her shoulders slumped. "I got up before dawn today to get the books," she said. "But the books were already gone! I knew who had to have them, because no other house had lights on. Trevor. I marched up to his house and stormed in without knocking, I was so mad. I found him in the kitchen. He'd already read three of the books. Stayed up all night reading, he had. And damaging those books. We got into a yelling match, but he only said, first come, first serve and then he told me to get out."

She heaved in a breath. "I was just. So. Angry. I didn't know what to do."

"So, you hurt his books," I said.

Swallowing, Mavis nodded. "I left him in the kitchen and headed for the door, but then I saw those books of his in the living room. I tiptoed in and before he could catch me, I broke the spines on all his favorites."

She stood there, her T-shirt suddenly limp on her shoulders. In the corner, Sergeant Thiessen had his notebook open and was writing furiously.

"And what happened then?" I asked quietly. Everyone else seemed to hold their breath.

"He came after me, of course." Her voice was small, barely audible. "He must have heard me, because he came tearing out of the kitchen and chased me out of the house. He was furious. He pushed me down and I grabbed the first thing my hand found to defend myself."

"One of Betty-Lynn's gnomes."

She nodded. "I hit him, and he collapsed on me. I guess I hit him too hard. He wasn't breathing and there was so much blood. I didn't know what to do so I shoved the gnome back into place and ran home. I was still showering when you called me to come help Betty-Lynn."

* * * *

After the shock of seeing Mavis led out and placed in the back of a police car, the neighbors grilled Betty-Lynn, Wilma, Tanzy, Sandra, and Dixey, demanding they disclose the juicy news. I stood by Betty-Lynn's front door with Sergeant Thiessen.

"You know, we would have gotten her eventually," he said, but there was a new respect in his voice. "Her fingerprints were likely all over that gnome and there would have been other forensic evidence."

"I know. But it would have taken a while and cost a whole lot of resources." I smiled up at him sweetly. "I thought I'd save you some time with a little book learning."

Before he could answer, I left him and headed down the driveway. After all, when the best detectives walk away into the sunset, they always leave their readers wanting more.

Author of the police procedural Detective Kazakov Mysteries and the amateur sleuth Phoebe Clay Mysteries, **Karen L. Abrahamson** writes fantasy, romance, and mystery. Her latest short fiction can be found in the anthology *Moonlight and Misadventure*, and in *Ellery Queen's Mystery Magazine* and *Black Cat Mystery Magazine*. When she isn't writing she can be found with a camera and backpack in fabulous locations around the world.

COLD CASE

BEV VINCENT

The man on the bench on Roger's front porch was almost certainly dead. He was sitting upright with his head tilted back, but through the panoramic viewfinder embedded in his door Roger could see what looked like ice crystals on the man's eyebrows and his facemask. It had gotten down to 9° Fahrenheit overnight—uncharacteristically frigid for Southeast Texas—and the four inches of snow that fell two days earlier still covered the lawn. Roger's home heating unit had been running constantly for the past twenty-four hours, trying to keep the Arctic blast at bay.

Roger wondered what to do. Go outside and check on the man? If it hadn't been freezing cold and they weren't in the middle of a pandemic, he might have. Better to remain inside, he decided. He thought about calling his friend Jim Sheppard, a retired police detective, for advice. But what if the man wasn't dead? Roger called 911 instead.

He watched through the kitchen window, a vantage point from which he kept track of the comings and goings in the neighborhood. It took a while. No doubt there were more pressing emergencies for the first responders to deal with in the middle of this historic cold spell, including house fires and hypothermia. He felt like he should have been doing something while he waited, but he couldn't bring himself to go outside until the EMTs arrived. For all he knew, the man might have died from COVID-19.

Nearly forty minutes after his 911 call, he heard a siren in the distance. Shortly thereafter, an ambulance pulled into his driveway, red lights pulsing. That was bound to cause a stir in this quiet neighborhood. He could imagine everyone going to their windows to see what was going on, just as he'd done often enough in the past. Now that he was retired and living alone, it seemed like he had nothing but time on his hands. If there weren't people to watch, he had a birdfeeder outside the kitchen window. The antics of the squirrels and birds were endlessly entertaining.

He bundled up in several layers of clothes—including two pairs of socks—and put on two masks. After watching the EMTs through the viewfinder for a while as they performed their preliminary examination, he opened the door and leaned out into the frigid morning air.

"Is he dead?"

One of the EMTs nodded gravely. "Do you know him?"

Roger stared at the body occupying his porch bench. The EMTs had pulled down the man's facemask while assessing him for signs of life. He looked to be about eighty, with shaggy gray hair and a deeply wrinkled face. "I don't think so."

"We're going to have to call the JP," the EMT said. "And the police. Suspicious death."

Roger took in what they were saying. Had someone killed this man? If so, why would they leave him on his front porch? In a book, it would be a warning, like the horse's head in *The Godfather*, but he didn't have dealings with people like that. It didn't make any sense.

He looked at the cobblestone path leading around the corner of his garage to the driveway, where the ambulance was idling, emitting gray gouts of exhaust. If the man—or whoever had deposited his body here—had made any tracks in the snow, they were gone now, trampled by the EMTs.

Rather than stand outside in the cold, he closed the door and went back into the kitchen to wait for the circus to come to town. The EMTs retreated to their ambulance, where it was presumably warm. He felt bad about not inviting them inside, but he couldn't take any risks. They interacted with sick people all the time.

In due course, several police cars arrived. There was also a passenger vehicle, driven by a woman Roger recognized as the justice of the peace, the only person who could officially declare the man dead. A white panel truck with "Crime Scene Unit" written on the side parked in the driveway across the street.

Roger left them to their business, stripping off a couple of layers of clothing. He watched the JP confer with the EMTs and sign something on a clipboard. While he waited for whatever was going to happen next, Roger texted his friends. At this time of morning, he would usually have been on his way to a nearby coffee shop to meet up with them, although they likely would have canceled today due to the cold weather. The coffee shop had been closed for months because of the pandemic, but there were still tables and benches outside and nobody seemed to mind if they used them. Everyone brought his own travel cup of coffee and they sat as far apart as possible without having to shout at each other, removing their masks only to drink.

Eventually someone knocked on his door. He put his masks and extra layers of clothing back on, quickly stepped outside and pulled the door closed behind him.

The detectives introduced themselves: Melrose and Hammond. Neither offered to shake hands, thankfully, and Roger was careful to maintain at least six feet of distance from them.

"I was hoping we could talk inside," Melrose said, rubbing his arms.

Roger shook his head. "Sorry. We'll have to do it out here."

"It's just that it's a little cold," Hammond said.

That was an understatement—it was freezing. Roger wondered whether there were virus particles in the clouds emanating from around the edges of the detectives' masks. As someone with a history of respiratory illnesses, he had been taking strict precautions for the past year. He had his groceries delivered rather than go in the store, and the only people he'd allowed into his house had been the repairmen who'd replaced his central AC and heater the previous summer—a system that was currently getting a serious workout. He didn't feel the need to share that information with the detectives, though.

"If an old guy like me can put up with it, I'm sure you young fellas can."

Hammond and Melrose exchanged glances. "We could always come back with a warrant," Melrose said.

Roger almost laughed. It was like a scene from a TV show—a badly written one at that. He looked at his watch. "I was supposed to be having coffee with Judge Raglan right about now. Do you want me to call him for you?"

Hammond sighed. "Okay, have it your way. Do you mind answering some questions?"

"Not at all."

"Do you know this man?" Hammond asked.

Roger had been deliberately looking anywhere but at the corpse sitting on his bench, but now he gave the body a closer look. There was something vaguely familiar about him, but he couldn't put his finger on it. "No. I don't think so."

"What do you think he's doing here?" Melrose asked.

Rather than give the inappropriate response that flashed through his mind, Roger simply shrugged. His ex-wife often said his smart mouth would get him into serious trouble someday.

"That thing in your front door," Melrose said, pointing at the panoramic viewfinder. "I don't suppose it records."

Roger shook his head. He'd seen the recent viral doorbell camera video of a distraught young woman who'd come to someone's door in the middle of the night in a nearby community, but he'd never found any reason to install one himself. Too many things were connected to the internet as it was these days.

Once they were finished with their questions, Roger asked a few of his own. He wasn't surprised to find they weren't forthcoming. If they knew who the man was, they weren't saying, nor would they offer any opinion as to how he had died. Nor could Roger read anything in their masked faces. They grumbled about how the EMTs had trampled their crime scene, as if it were Roger's fault. After a while, they said he could go. When Hammond offered him a business card, Roger told him to stick it in the door jamb after he was inside.

He went back into the kitchen and watched the CSIs process the scene. Eventually they summoned the EMTs, who bundled the dead man onto a stretcher. He seemed to be frozen stiff, so it was an awkward process.

The police cars were still parked out front as officers went door to door, canvassing the neighbors. Roger read a lot of crime fiction and regularly watched Nordic series on Netflix, so he was familiar with the process. No doubt the pandemic made investigating crimes more difficult, what with social distancing and all, and this brutally cold weather wouldn't help. Who wanted to open their doors and let out their precious heat?

He removed his outer layers and headed toward the cubbyhole where his computer was located. On the way, he surveyed the house, which looked like it had been ransacked by a burglar searching for valuables. All the cabinet doors beneath sinks stood wide open to help prevent the pipes from freezing. So far, he'd been lucky, although he'd heard from a few friends who were dealing with burst pipes and no running water.

He opened Zoom and clicked on Ashley Paton's name on his contact list. She was a single mother who had moved into the house across the street a few weeks after Roger's ex-wife moved out. Before the pandemic, they had been nodding acquaintances, but they'd connected last fall when she posted on the Nextdoor app, looking for assistance with her teenage daughter's science homework. Roger, who had a degree in chemistry and plenty of spare time, had volunteered to help the harried mom and her remote-learning daughter. They'd struck up a virtual friendship, talking a couple of evenings a week after his online tutorials with Lizzie, usually over glasses of wine.

It took Ashley a few minutes to answer, but Roger was used to that. She looked frazzled but offered a wry smile. "So, they finally caught up with you," she said.

"Who?"

"The cops. I always figured you were really a wanted felon hiding out under an assumed name."

"Did you, now?"

"Yeah. Someone like DB Sweeney. With a trove of stolen cash."

"Because I'm obviously living the high life."

"Obviously," she said. "Maybe someday you'll wise up and take me away from all this." She liked to tease him, but he knew she only did so because she thought he was safe. Too old to worry about.

"So, what's the scuttlebutt on the street?" he asked.

"They're saying someone died on your front porch," she said.

"That's all?" he asked. "No juicy tidbits or rumors? Theories about who he was?"

"Nothing yet," she said. "Give it time."

"Did you talk to the police?"

"They came to the door, but I couldn't be bothered to mask up and deal with them. Lizzie was in a mood, and that was all I could handle at the moment. Besides, I didn't see anything, so what would be the point?"

Roger nodded. "Didn't you install one of those video doorbells? You know, after you thought someone stole your Amazon parcel?"

"Someone might have."

"But it was just delivered to the wrong house."

"That beeyotch." Ashley looked over her shoulder, presumably to make sure her daughter wasn't listening. "Took her nearly a week to bring it over. It's all because of those funky street numbers we have," she said. "What were the developers thinking? Sixes look like eights and fives look like sixes. Someone should do something about that."

He let her run out of steam—it was a familiar complaint. "But your camera still works, right?"

"Yeah."

“Your front door is directly across from my driveway. Anyone passing by on the street might trigger it.”

Her mouth dropped open. “Oh. Right. Let me see.”

Roger watched as she clicked and dragged and cursed and licked her lips.

“OK, I’ve got it.”

“Can you send it to me? Everything from, let’s say, eight o’clock last night until eight this morning.”

“You’re lucky Lizzie is off school today because of the storm. Otherwise, you would’ve had to wait until later. I can’t get near the computer during the daytime Monday through Friday.”

“I’m a lucky guy, ” Roger said.

“Luckier than whoever dropped dead on your front porch, that’s for sure.”

While the video file from his neighbor’s door camera was downloading, he went online to see if the incident had made the news. So far there was no mention of it, other than some people on Nextdoor asking what all the police activity had been about. Then he made a pot of tea, returned to his computer and found a Chick Corea playlist on Spotify.

The sensor that activated Ashley’s camera was sensitive enough to be triggered by every passing car and anyone out walking their dog or taking a stroll. He was surprised by the amount of traffic on the street, considering the late hour, the terrible road conditions, and the cold. Roger sometimes felt like he was living in a different reality from people who were still going out to bars and restaurants or movies. The kinds of people, he felt, who were responsible for the epidemic lasting as long as it had.

Watching the footage was nowhere near as captivating as they made it out to be on the cops shows he liked. After a while, he clicked Pause, stretched, reheated his neglected tea in the microwave, and called his friend Jim Sheppard. He was surprised the retired cop hadn’t called him after receiving his earlier text message.

“Roger. What’s going on?”

“That’s what I was calling to ask you. I figured you would have called some of your old buddies to get the inside scoop by now.”

There was a long pause before Sheppard answered. “Maybe I did.”

“What did you find out? Do they know who the guy was? How he died?”

“I’m not supposed to say anything,” Sheppard said. “You’re kind of a person of interest.”

“Me?”

“Not letting the detectives into your house kinda made them mad. You did find a dead body. On your front porch. You know as well as I do that the person who calls in something like that is often involved.”

“That’s only on TV. Wait a second. If I’m a person of interest, that must mean he didn’t die of natural causes, right?”

“Well...” Sheppard drew the word out. “I’m not saying that.”

“Do they know who he is?”

"Not yet. He had no ID on him. Not much of anything, in fact. Not even keys or a cell phone. They're hoping to get a hit on his prints or DNA. It'll take a while. Things are backed up because of the power outages."

"Cause of death?"

Sheppard sighed. "Too soon to say."

"Did he die here or somewhere else?"

"Unclear. The coroner is backed up, too. All these exposure deaths, not to mention the carbon monoxide poisonings."

Roger shook his head. "Coldest stretch we've had in half a century, people without electricity or water for days, and still folks are out there killing each other." He took a deep breath. "But how did he end up on my porch?"

"No clue. And no one's calling it murder. Not yet. But listen, Roger, you can't tell anyone I said anything."

"My lips are sealed," Roger said. "Anyhow, talk to you later. I have to check out some surveillance video."

"What's that? Roger, who's always ranting about the surveillance state, has a doorbell camera? And why didn't the cops get that from you?"

"I only said I didn't want one of those voice-activated home assistants listening in on everything. Anyway, it's not my camera—it belongs to one of my neighbors."

"Not that pretty little thang across the street?"

"Lips sealed, Jim—not just for you."

"I should warn you against tampering with evidence."

"It's not evidence unless I find something. And even then, it's just a copy of evidence—the original is still there if the cops want it. Gotta go."

He returned to the computer and pressed Play, taking a sip of tea that had already cooled. The power had been out for nearly twelve hours two days earlier. After it came back on, he'd followed the power company's request to reduce thermostats to 68° to help protect the electric grid. He'd been surprised by how quickly things grew cold at that temperature.

It didn't take long for him to find something on Ashley's surveillance video that made him grope for the mouse to press Pause. He rewound a few seconds and watched again. Thanks to the solar-powered lights his ex-wife had insisted they install along both sides of the driveway to keep her from going off the edge of the culvert into the ditch, Roger was able to see the silhouette of a man who was moving down the street unsteadily, lurching more than walking.

When he reached Roger's driveway, the man paused for a moment, looked around, then turned in and shambled toward the house. A few seconds later, he moved out of frame, presumably arriving at Roger's front door. What had he done then? The time code said it was shortly after ten o'clock. Roger hadn't heard anyone at the door. By then, he would have been tucked into bed, reading a novel on his iPad. The bedroom was the warmest room in the house, but even without the big chill to deal with, he was usually in bed by nine thirty at the latest.

He made a note of the time on the pad beside his computer. He wouldn't volunteer the information to anyone else without seeking Ashley's permission first. He was just about to send her a message when his computer chimed, indicating the arrival of email.

When he clicked over to the mail application, he saw that it was a "found dog" notification from Nextdoor. Most of the messages he received from that site either reported a lost pet or a stray someone had found. He was about to delete it when he noticed that the dog had been found on his street last evening. He opened the email and read further.

There was a picture of the dog along with a phone number to call if anyone recognized it. It had showed up, shivering and barking, at the poster's door at around 9:45 last night. They had fed and watered the animal. If no one contacted them in the next day or two, they planned to take it to a vet to see if there was an embedded chip.

Something Ashley said earlier made Roger wonder. He pulled up Zoom and clicked her name. She showed up on his screen a minute later.

"Wow, twice in one day. To what do I owe this honor? Did you get the video I sent?"

"I did," he said. "Thanks for that."

"Did you find anything?"

"I think so. Are you doing anything right now?"

"Trying to decide what to feed the beast for supper. Why? What did you have in mind?"

"How'd you like to go for a walk?"

Ashley sat up straight and rubbed the side of her head. "Well, now. That's a surprise."

"Don't worry. My intentions are pure."

She made a face. "Ah, you disappoint me. I was hoping for something impure. Isn't it a little cold for a promenade, though?"

"I thought you might enjoy helping me solve a mystery. After all, you provided a couple of the clues."

"Did I? How intriguing."

"Well, the video, for one. If you go to 10:07 last night, you'll see someone walking down the street and entering my driveway. So now we know when he arrived at my front door."

"I suppose I should tell someone about this."

"Eventually," Roger said. "First, we need to take a walk."

"Oh, please don't drag me away from the teenage monster who's been lumbering around the house all day long complaining about everything."

"Dress warmly," Roger said.

He suited up for the third time in a few hours. Outside, he picked Hammond's business card up from the welcome mat, where it landed when he opened the front door. He didn't even glance at the bench. He was pretty sure he was going to have to replace it. It wasn't that he ever sat on it, but that was where delivery people usually left his groceries and packages. The fact that a man had died there made it feel creepy.

By the time he reached the end of his driveway, Ashley had emerged from her house. She was so bundled up, she reminded him of the Peanuts cartoon where Charlie Brown had on so many winter clothes that when he fell over he couldn't get back up again. "Is that really you in there?" he asked.

"I can see you," she said. "Undressing me with your eyes."

"That'd be a job," Roger said, hoping she couldn't see him blush.

She chuckled. "Okay, wise guy. What's the plan?"

"What did you say a while ago when I asked you about your doorbell camera?"

She frowned. "That I'd check it out and send it to you?"

"No, before that. We talked about the time you thought someone stole your package."

"Don't get me started."

"You mentioned how confusing the street numbers are. How the sixes look like eights, and the—"

"—and the fives look like sixes, and the eights look like zeroes."

"Right. Coupled with the fact that there are only about three different designs for the houses on the street."

"Still not following you."

"So, suppose you're out late at night, and maybe you're on the old side."

"Older than you?"

"A little. And it's really, really cold and maybe you're feeling frantic and you get disoriented."

"Okay."

"You get turned around. And then you see a house that looks exactly like yours and the number makes sense…as far as the numbers on this street make any sense…so you sigh. You're home. Except the front door won't open."

"He went to your door thinking it was his?"

Roger nodded. "When he couldn't get in, he sat on the bench and died—either from a heart attack or exposure."

"That's so sad," Ashley said.

"I'm willing to bet we'll find his front door unlocked."

"Why?"

"Because he didn't plan to be outside very long. No keys or phone."

"Why was he out that late on such a cold night in the first place?"

"Because his dog got loose."

"His dog?"

"He must have opened the door for some reason—maybe he was checking for a delivery, or maybe he just wanted to look at the snow, I don't know. But Fido got loose, and he couldn't leave him out in this weather, so he went looking for him."

"And you know all of this from my doorbell video?"

"That and a post on Nextdoor by some people up the street who found a stray dog last night."

"So you think…?"

"My house is number 65."

"Sure…and I'm in 64."

"If sixes look like eights and fives look like sixes…"

"He lives in number 86?"

"Or something like that."

They were trudging down the ice- and snow-covered street. Ashley stopped and turned to look up at him. "Not that I don't mind getting out of the house and all, but why did you need me to come along?"

"To be my witness. Corroborate my story. The police think I might have been involved in the man's death."

"Okay," she said. "I'll testify on your behalf at your murder trial."

Roger smirked. "Gee. Thanks."

As they continued down the street in silence, Roger mused about how well he knew the neighbors within a certain radius of his house but, beyond that, everyone was more or less a stranger. A few he might recognize if he saw them somewhere else, but not many. The man on his front porch had probably lived less than a dozen houses down the block, but he'd only looked vaguely familiar. Of course, people didn't look the same in death as they did in life.

But still.

When they reached number 86, Roger noticed two sets of tracks in the driveway—those from a dog and those from a man, both heading away from the house into the street. He went to the front door and reached for the knob. Before he could turn it, Ashley asked, "Shouldn't you knock?"

He did. They waited for a full minute, shifting their weigh from foot to foot to keep warm. When no one answered, he gripped the knob and tried to turn it. The door opened. He turned to Ashley. "Remember…you're my witness."

She nodded and followed him inside.

It felt weird to be in a stranger's house. Roger hadn't been inside many places for the past year. He called out, "Anyone home?" He was confident no one would answer, though.

"Look here," Ashley said, pointing to a wall covered with photographs. "Recognize anyone?"

Roger scanned the pictures. Most were of younger adults with children, but a few featured an older couple. Roger tapped one. "That's him."

Ashley picked up an envelope from a table near the entrance to the living room. "Charles Kent," she read.

Roger nodded. "And there's the killer," he said, pointing at a picture of a dog that resembled the one from the Nextdoor posting. He pulled out his cell phone and dialed the number printed on the bottom of Hammond's business card.

"Detective Hammond? Roger Acker. Yes, that's right. I know the name of the man who died on my front porch," he said. "And I think I can explain what happened to him. Yes, I'll be back home by then. No, you can't come in, so dress warmly." He ended the call and turned to Ashley. Even with her mask and snug-fitting hat and hood, he could see that she looked sad.

"Poor man," she said. "Living all alone with his dog."

Roger frowned, wondering if she was thinking about him when she said this. "Where's the rest of his family?" he asked. "Why weren't they worried about him?"

"Busy lives," she said. "And it's been less than a day. Do your kids check up on you every day?"

He shook his head. "Once a week, if I'm lucky. More like twice a month. Let's get out of here."

They trudged back up the street. When they reached their houses, they turned to face each other, standing six feet apart. "If I invited you to dinner some evening, would you come over?" Ashley asked.

"When I get my second vaccine dose, sure, I'd like that."

"Lizzie likes you, and I think she'd be happy to have someone besides me to be cranky at."

"I'll let you know what the cops say," he said.

"Let me know the trial date, too," she said, wrinkling up her nose so he could tell she was grinning. She turned toward her driveway, stopped, and turned back. "I wonder what'll happen to his dog."

Roger shrugged. "I'm allergic, so he can't come live with me."

"Allergic, huh? I'll keep that in mind. Let me know when you get your shot."

"Will do. See you on the computer."

He continued to his front porch and stared at the bench. After a few seconds, he shrugged and sat down, waiting for Hammond and Melrose to arrive.

✗

Bev Vincent (bevvincent.com) is the author of *Stephen King: A Complete Exploration of His Work, Life, and Influences*, as well as more than 120 short stories, including appearances in *Ellery Queen's, Alfred Hitchcock's* and *Black Cat Mystery Magazines*, and *Cemetery Dance*. His work has been published in twenty languages and nominated for the Stoker (twice), Edgar, Ignotus and ITW Thriller Awards. In 2018, he co-edited the anthology *Flight or Fright* with Stephen King. Recent works include the novellas "The Ogilvy Affair" and "The Dead of Winter," the latter found in *Dissonant Harmonies* with Brian Keene.

LOOT AND LOVE

JOHNSTON McCULLEY

CHAPTER I

THIEVES AT WORK

Standing on the corner, brushed by the home-hurrying crowd of workers, Gus Slatten struck a match and cupped his hands to light the cigarette he had just rolled. He glanced over his cupped hands across the street and down it for a short distance, at the front of Belstein's jewelry store and pawnshop.

Gus Slatten was known as an inveterate cigarette smoker, and he had rolled countless thousands of them; but it appeared that his skill was dormant this evening. The cigarette he was lighting came undone, the tobacco was spilled into his hands and went through his fingers to the walk. Gus Slatten cursed softly beneath his breath, yawned, and reached into pockets for tobacco sack and papers once more.

He stepped out closer to the edge of the curb, straddled a fire hydrant, and started rolling another. He glanced up and down the street as he worked, as though overcome by boredom. He took his own good time about rolling the cigarette.

When it was finished, he struck another match, cupped his hands again, and lighted his smoke. Once more he looked over his cupped hands at the Belstein pawnshop and jewelry store. This time he saw what he had wished to see—old Belstein locking the front door of his establishment.

Tossing the burned match into the gutter, Gus Slatten puffed a couple of times, inhaled, yawned again, and marched slowly to the corner and across the street through the hurrying traffic. It was a few minutes after six o'clock in the evening. Belstein, it was evident, had tarried over his books. But now he was shuffling up the street toward the two rooms he called home. Gus Slatten knew all about Belstein and his habits.

Safe across the street, Slatten entered a tobacco shop on the corner and purchased another sack of tobacco. He engaged the clerk in conversation.

"Me for some eats," said Gus Slatten, "and then for a little poker game around the corner, unless I take a notion to go home and read the papers. This is gettin' to be a dead town if a man don't like the movies."

"Ain't it the truth!" the clerk replied.

"I've quit seven jobs in six months just because they get on my nerves," Slatten continued. "A man can't seem to settle down anymore."

"Ain't it the truth!"

"I've a notion to get me a stake and tear out of this country and into some live one—but gettin' a stake ain't the easiest thing in the world these days."

"Ain't it the truth!"

"Boy, put on a new record!" Gus Slatten advised. "That one is gettin' rusty." He grinned and left the tobacco shop, and once more he stood for an instant at the curb, yawning for the benefit of a plain-clothes man who was passing. Then Gus Slatten started walking up the street slowly against the tide of pedestrian traffic, keeping close to the fronts of the buildings. He approached the Belstein establishment and merely glanced inside through the windows without turning his head. It was a rapid glance, too, but it showed Slatten that everything was as it should be.

On along the street he went until he came to the next corner. There he saw Henry Burl approaching, and he stopped to light his cigarette again, though the cigarette did not need lighting. Henry Burl passed within two feet of him.

"All right!" Burl grunted, without looking at Gus Slatten, and then walked on.

Gus Slatten yawned again and continued on as though he had no interest at all either in Henry Burl or the Belstein jewelry store and pawnshop.

It might be well to describe Gus Slatten as a medium-sized man dressed inconspicuously. He was an ordinary-looking individual who would not have attracted attention in a crowd. Attracting attention was something Gus Slatten did not crave.

His eyes were small and expressionless. His mouth had lines of cruelty around the corners of it. A student of the human countenance would have looked at Gus Slatten once and then felt his pockets to be sure that his watch and purse remained with him.

Henry Burl was a large man, with too much fat on his frame. There was a look of frankness in his face, and it caused some men to have confidence in Henry Burl. Having gained a man's confidence, Burl knew how to turn it to profit.

They made an excellent pair, one having certain qualities that the other did not. The police had their suspicions, but they were nothing more than suspicions as yet. Both men held jobs now and then for a short time. They were not together much. And when they did meet, it was as casual acquaintances.

Gus Slatten, having progressed against the evening throng for a distance of three blocks, turned into a side street and finally made his way into an alley and started back through it in the direction from which he had come.

The alley was used by pedestrians during the morning and evening rush hours, so the presence of Slatten in it did not cause any comment. He walked along at an ordinary rate of speed as though attending strictly to his own business, and as though that business was an honest one. He seemed preoccupied.

As a matter of fact, Gus Slatten never had been more alert than he was at that particular moment.

He came to the street nearest the rear of the Belstein store, crossed it, and continued down the alley. But in the alley on this block there were no pedestrians, for it was blind at the other end. Slatten did not go all the way to the rear door of the Belstein establishment. He stopped one building before it. He opened a door there and entered the rear of a pool and billiard hall.

The place was crowded at that hour, which was what Gus Slatten expected and was glad to see. He sat down with his back to the wall, rolled another cigarette, and watched the men playing at the nearest table. An observer would have said that Slatten was waiting for some friend to come along and propose a game.

Henry Burl entered from the front, spoke to a few acquaintances, and finally made his way to the rear, where he stood against the wall within three feet of Gus Slatten, his arms folded across his chest, his feet crossed, a picture of innocent loafing.

The conversation was conducted from the corners of the mouths of the two men, and a third man standing six feet away could not have heard it.

"Well?" Slatten asked.

"All right, like I said, Gus. Belstein went right to his rooms. I could smell supper cookin'. His old woman opened the door and let him in."

"Then we'd better get busy, I suppose?"

"Surest thing you know, Gus. It's a good idea, if you're askin' me. This is the safest hour of the day."

"All right!"

That was all Gus Slatten said. Henry Burl yawned and walked away, not briskly, however. He stopped at one of the tables and watched for a moment, engaged a friend in conversation, and presently made his way to the front door and the street.

Gus Slatten got up from the chair and stretched his arms. He glanced around swiftly and then crossed the rear of the wide room toward the alley door. Boldness was the thing, he kept telling himself. Simply be bold and avoid being seen—that was all that was necessary.

He opened the door, stepped into the alley, and closed the door behind him. Lighting a cigarette again, he looked over his cupped hands and made sure that there was nobody coming in from the street. Then he walked briskly a distance of twenty feet and was at the rear door of the Belstein place.

There was a little doorway into which a man could step. Gus Slatten stepped into it and glanced through the glass with its protection of steel bars. He could see the rear of the Belstein store, but not through to the street in front.

He took a key from his pocket, inserted it in the lock, turned it, and heard the tumblers of the lock snap back. Gus Slatten grinned. He had been at some trouble and expense to get that particular key, and he was glad to find that it worked well and came up to his expectations.

But there was a bolt on the inside of the door, too. However, that did not bother Slatten. He put out his head and glanced up the alley again, then stepped back, hurled himself forward, and snapped the bolt out of the wood casement. An instant later he was inside the store.

He used the key again to lock the door. If the watchman did happen to make his rounds ahead of time, he would try the door, find it locked, and go on his way after a glance inside the place. And that glance would show him nothing wrong!

Crouching down behind the door, Gus Slatten watched and waited. He could not be seen from the front, and he could not be seen from the rear. Burl, he knew, would have to circle the block, and that would take time, especially since Burl would speak to every man he knew and prepare an alibi of a sort.

But after a time there came a peculiar tap on the door. Gus Slatten stood up and peered through the glass, turned the key and opened the door, and let Burl slip inside. He immediately locked the door again.

"Good enough!" he grunted.

"Let's work fast," Burl said.

"Plenty of time. The watchman won't be around for more than an hour. He's due here at seven-thirty. We'll wait until he has gone on and then slip out. Nobody would think of a trick bein' pulled at this hour. Broad daylight or the middle of the night—that's the regular old stuff. Best time in the world is the supper hour, when everybody is glad the day's work is done and is relaxin'."

"Uh-huh!" said Burl.

"Come ahead!"

They slipped through another door and came to a sort of cage of steel. The gate in the cage was fastened with a padlock. Gus Slatten was ready for that, too. He took another key from his pocket and unlocked the gate. They darted inside.

The place was in semigloom. In front there was a safe with a single incandescent light burning before it. But they did not intend to touch that safe.

"Gloves!" Slatten whispered.

They took thin rubber gloves from their pockets and pulled them on. They did not intend to leave their cards in the shape of fingerprints.

For a moment they crouched behind the counter and listened. No sound reached their ears save the distant rumbling of traffic in the street.

"Safe enough!" Burl whispered. "But let's be careful, Gus. If we make a good haul, we don't want anything bad to happen afterward."

"Losin' your nerve?" Slatten asked.

"I don't lose my nerve on a job, and you know it!"

"Then don't make that line of talk. Just remember our plans and carry 'em out. That's all that's necessary."

Gus Slatten and Burl knew some things about the Belstein establishment that other folks did not know. They had been keeping an eye on the place for some time. Belstein complained that he was a pawnbroker just managing to make his rent and living expenses, but Gus Slatten and Burl knew that he was growing rich. He purchased diamonds at ridiculous prices, sometimes from men and women who had to sell them to get funds quickly, and sometimes without asking too many questions. He kept a few of these diamonds for sale, but the greater number were marketed uptown from a pretentious jewelry store, this store getting them through a wholesaler with whom Belstein had shady dealings.

And Belstein had certain jewels that he did not keep in his regular safe. Beneath this counter he had a small safe hidden behind a panel. In it was a fortune in gems.

Gus Slatten got the panel back and exposed the safe. He knelt before it, and Henry Burl stepped back to one side of the cage and listened intently. Slatten was a good safe man, though the police did not know it.

Slatten and Burl had done many things during the past two years that had puzzled the police. Some of their deeds had been credited to other and better-known crooks. Time after time some detective or plain-clothes man had suspected the pair or one of them, but his investigation always had come to naught. Slatten and Burl had been lucky.

Now Slatten set to work on the safe and soon had it open. His grunt caused Burl to look around. Slatten was pulling out tiny drawers, and in each tiny drawer were at least half a dozen fine jewels.

"Rich!" he whispered.

"We'll have to keep 'em out of sight for a time," Burl said.

"Of course! That was the plan. We can hold in for a couple of months, I guess, and then fence 'em and have a get-away stake that will amount to somethin'."

Slatten took a small bag of chamois from one of his pockets and poured the jewels into it. He emptied all the little drawers.

"Wonder if there's anything else we can pick up?" he said.

"We'd better stick to our original plans," Burl replied, with some show of nervousness. "We'll get into trouble if we start to prowlin' around here. I'm no white liver, but I feel shaky in here for some reason."

"Don't be a fool! No burglar alarm attached to this thing." Slatten said. "Old Belstein didn't want anybody to know about this little safe behind the panel. He's a crook the same as we are."

"Let's call it a day," Burl said.

"I'll close the safe and panel. It'll delay the shock to the old boy for a few minutes," Slatten replied.

He closed the door of the safe, replaced the panel, slipped the bag of jewels into one of his hip pockets, and tore off his gloves and put them into another pocket.

"You'd better keep those gloves on," said Burl. "You might leave a print on the casement somewhere, or on that cage stuff."

"You make me sick!" Slatten whispered.

"Let's get out of here!"

"It's only seven twenty-five," Slatten told him. "In five minutes, if he is on time, that watchman will be at the back door. Want to open it in his face, you boob? He's generally on time to the dot, too. A man could set a watch by him. If watchmen weren't quite so regular in their habits, it'd be tougher for crooks."

"We've got to wait until he's tried the door and gone on?"

"Certainly! And for about ten minutes after that. The alley will be pitch dark by that time, too. Don't lose your nerve, Burl! Just stick to our plans. I'm goin' to roll a cigarette and take a smoke."

"For Heaven's sake don't do that!"

"Why not?"

"That crazy kind of tobacco you use! It smells different! If anything happened and the cops got in here in time to smell stale smoke—"

"You certainly are the careful little birdie this evenin'," Gus Slatten said.

He started to roll the cigarette. Burl growled something and went back to the gate of the steel cage. But Slatten did not light the cigarette. From the front of the store came a sound that caused him to thrust the cigarette into his pocket and step swiftly toward Burl.

"What's that?" he whispered.

Burl turned toward him a face that showed deathly white in the gathering gloom.

"It's Belstein!" he whispered. "He's come back to the store for somethin'!"

CHAPTER II

MISS LIZZIE ENTERS

Gus Slatten darted up beside Burl and looked around the corner of the cage and counter. He could see old Belstein hobbling from the front door toward the rear of the establishment. He carried an account book beneath one arm.

"Came back to fix his books!" Slatten whispered. "Tough luck!"

"What are we goin' to do?" Burl gasped. "We haven't time to lock the cage and get to the back door. And if we do that, the watchman will be there just in time to see us!"

Slatten growled something that Burl could not understand and thrust him quickly aside. He looked around the corner of the counter again. There was no chance, he saw, of darting away without being seen and recognized. Belstein knew him and Henry Burl, too. They had visited him often during the past three months, pawning things and redeeming them so as to get acquainted with Belstein and his shop and so make their plans for the robbery. And if Belstein recognized them now!

"Gus!" Burl whispered.

"Shut up!" Slatten warned. "Let me handle this!"

Belstein stopped beside one of the showcases and inspected the layout of cheap articles there. And then he continued toward the rear of the store. Slatten was sure, now, that Belstein intended to enter the cage, sit up at the counter, and fix his books. There was no escape.

And the watchman was due at the back door at that moment. To slip into that little rear hall would mean that the watchman might glance through the barred glass of the door and see them. They could not do that.

Gus Slatten never had been cornered before. And now fear came to him for the first time since he had started on his criminal career. He visualized the big prison up the river, the grim, gray walls, the guards, himself a convict. He saw red for an instant. Old Belstein was the man who could bring that to pass—if he ever spoke!

"Gus—" Burl whispered again.

"Silence, fool!" Slatten growled.

Slatten had made up his mind how to act in this emergency, but he knew better than to speak to Burl about it now. He knew that Burl would protest.

Belstein had almost reached the end of the counter. He stepped around it and saw at the first glance that the gate in the cage was open. The old man stopped, and a gurgle came from his throat. Then he gave a little cry of fear and darted forward rapidly.

Gus Slatten had picked up from the end of the counter a long, heavy piece of bronze, probably broken from some old work of art. It was his intention to strike once and quickly, to render the old man unconscious before he could recognize them.

But Belstein, rushing toward the place where he had stored his valuables, swayed to one side, and Slatten's blow missed. At the same instant Belstein glanced toward him.

"Slatten!" he cried.

Slatten saw red again. He had been recognized, and nothing could save him from the term in prison now, if Belstein lived to speak. He sprang forward. His left hand gripped the old man by the throat and choked back the second cry he would have given—a shout for help. The heavy piece of bronze described an arc through the air—then crashed home!

Belstein slumped to the floor. His body twitched and then was still. Slatten stood over him, scarcely realizing what he had done. He knew that Henry Burl was standing beside him. He heard Burl's horrified whisper as though from a far distance:

"Gus, you've killed him!"

Slatten realized it suddenly. He stooped and made sure. He was cool and collected in that instant, with a sort of peculiar reaction to his recent fright.

"Yes!" he grunted. "He recognized us, Burl. There was nothing else to do."

"But it's—it's murder—the chair!"

"Stop it, fool! Pull yourself together. We leave him here and go right ahead with our plans, only we'll have to be more careful now, of course. Stop and think! It's a cinch that these stones we have aren't listed. We can dispose of 'em probably without 'em ever bein' traced to the Belstein store. Buck up!"

Burl fought to do so, but he was trembling.

"Just forget about this and consider that we haven't done anything except get the stones like we planned to do," Slatten said. He took out his watch and glanced at it. "That watchman has come and gone," he added. "Let's get out of here. Remember the rest of our plans and carry 'em out!"

"All right!" Burl gulped.

He followed Slatten into the little rear hall. It was dark outside now. They hesitated for a moment, listening and watching. They crept on to the rear door and crouched behind it. Slatten stood up slowly and peered into the dark alley. He could see nothing, could hear nobody. He turned the key in the lock, opened the door a few inches, and finally stepped into the doorway. He was back instantly.

"Safe enough!" he whispered. "I saw the watchman just turnin' into the street. Get goin', Burl, and remember the scheme."

Henry Burl slipped noiselessly into the darkness and started down the alley. Gus Slatten slipped after him, stopped to lock the door, and went swiftly toward the rear door of the pool and billiard hall again.

He entered as he had done before. The place was still crowded, and no man gave him special attention. He sat in the same chair he had used before.

Ten minutes later, after rolling a cigarette with hands that did not shake at all, he arose, yawned, and stretched his arms, then addressed an acquaintance who stood at the nearest table.

"This is too quiet for me!" he declared. "I'm goin' to my room and read the papers and get some sleep. I was intendin' to sit into a poker game, but maybe it'd be cheaper to stay out."

The acquaintance grinned at him, and Gus Slatten walked slowly through the place and to the front door. He went out upon the street and stopped to roll and light another cigarette, just to show that he was his regular self. Patrolman Sam Kenbolt, making his monotonous rounds, stepped up beside him.

"Hello, Gus!" he said.

"Evenin', officer. Keepin' you busy?" Gus asked.

"Things are pretty quiet."

"I'll say that they are. I've been half asleep in that pool hall for an hour. Now I'm goin' to my room and read the papers and go to sleep. This town is gettin' dead."

"You working now?" Officer Renbolt asked.

"I am startin' tomorrow mornin'. Got me a job on the dock," Slatten replied.

"That's good stuff, Gus. A man better get a job and stick to it these days."

"Sometimes I think I'll go out West and turn cow-puncher," Gus answered. "Them boys get a little excitement, anyway."

The patrolman smiled and walked on, and as soon as his back was turned Gus Slatten sneered. Then he started off down the street, turned the first corner, walked three blocks to a cheap lodging house, ascended to the third floor, and was in his room.

He snapped on the single electric light the room boasted and locked the door. He put his hat over the keyhole, made sure that the shade at the one window was drawn down its full length, and then removed the bag of jewels from his hip pocket. Into the bag with the gems he slipped the two keys he had used.

In a corner of the room, after he had moved his bed, Gus Slatten lifted the loose end of a board. He had been at some trouble to fix it just the way he wanted it. He dropped the bag into a little hole beneath the board and slipped the board back into place. Working swiftly, he smeared dust around the edges of the board he had removed.

It was still loose, but Gus Slatten had prepared for that. He took a nail from his pocket, adjusted it in the proper place, and reached for an old iron paperweight that somebody had left in the room long before. And then he began singing at the top of his voice.

Slatten had been singing that way each evening for quite a time, preparing the way for just this emergency. As he reached a particularly loud and high note, he smashed at the nail with the paperweight. Two smashes, and the nail was driven home.

He had to repeat this with another nail, and then, continuing his singing, he looked at the job closely. The heads of the nails were bright where his blows had landed. Slatten growled, took another nail from his pocket, rubbed rust from it, mixed it with dust from the floor, and rubbed the bright heads of the nails he had driven.

He inspected the job again and grinned. He slipped the bed back into place, then glanced around to see that everything was as it should be.

Now he removed coat and vest and rolled up the sleeves of his shirt. He took his hat from the door and put it on the table. He removed his shoes, settled himself in a chair beneath the light, opened an evening paper, turned to the sporting page, and began reading like some honest workman gleaning the day's news before going to bed.

For half an hour he read, and then there came a knock at the door. Gus Slatten arose, tossed the paper aside, stepped across the room, and turned the key. He opened the door promptly.

"Oh! Hello, Burl!" he exclaimed. "Come on in! I'm takin' it easy tonight."

"Good idea!" Henry Burl said.

He stepped inside, and Slatten closed the door again but did not lock it. He motioned Burl to a chair and sat down himself.

"Well, Burl, what's the good word?" he asked.

"I don't know any news."

"I'm startin' work in the mornin' down at the dock," Slatten said, in a loud voice. "Maybe I can find you a job down there, if you want one."

"I want one, all right."

Their voices gradually were growing softer. Had anybody been listening, they would have thought that this was merely idle conversation between two acquaintances. But suddenly Burl leaned across the little table and spoke in a whisper.

"Gus! I'm afraid that—"

"Hush!" Slatten whispered. "Keep talking in an ordinary mumblin' tone. Then nobody can understand what we say. But don't whisper. What about it?"

"I don't think they've discovered it yet."

"Mean to say that you've been hangin' around there?"

"I—I wanted to see if they—"

"You fool! That's the way they catch men, when they go back to the scene of the crime to see what's doin'. For Heaven's sake have common sense! You stay away from there and be surprised when you hear it. Act like you didn't know anything about it and didn't care much."

"I—I'm afraid, Gus! I never expected anything like what happened."

"Neither did I, you fool. But it had to be done, didn't it? Either that or go up the river for ten or fifteen years. You didn't want to do that, did you? All right, then!"

"Maybe we'd better blow, Gus."

"You are a fool! That'd be about the same as telephonin' the cops at headquarters to come and get us because we did it."

"I didn't do it—you did!"

"Little innocent! We were pals and went there to rob, didn't we? Makes no difference if I did strike the blow—you were in on it!"

"If we could get away—"

"Don't be a fool, I said! The best thing is to stay right here and act natural. We'll never be suspected. And in a couple of months, we can sell the stones, and then we can drift out of town easy like and go somewhere else and live like two princes. Don't think about the thing so much. Forget it!"

"I—I never can forget it, Gus!"

"See here!" Slatten exclaimed. "When a man gets to feelin' that way, he's liable to tip off somethin'. You buck up, now! Everything'll be all right, I tell you! Get your nerve back! Look at me—I actually did it, and I'm as cool as a man could be. Talk about something else!" Slatten raised his voice again. "Did you notice what a wallopin' the Giants gave Pittsburg today?" he asked. "Wish I'd seen that game!"

"There's a good fight next week," Burl said, trying to get into the game. "Don't talk baseball. It—it reminds me of diamonds, and they remind me of—"

"Stop it!" Slatten hissed. "Talk about somethin' else! You're the limit!"

Burl gulped and tried. "I hope I can get me a job," he said. "I need one. I'm about broke, and my room rent is due. If I get me another job, I'll hang onto it, you can bet."

"That's the stuff!" Slatten said. "I'm startin' in at the dock in the mornin', Burl, and I'll ask the foreman if he can use another good man. Maybe I can get you work down there. The pay's good, even if the work is hard. And it's steady, too. In a few weeks you'd be on your feet and goin' strong."

"You ask him," Burl said.

"All right! You come down about the middle of the afternoon, and we'll see what happens," Slatten replied.

There came a timid tap at the door.

"Come in!" Gus Slatten called.

The door was opened easily. A woman's head was put in. Her thin voice reached their ears.

"I don't remember whether I left your towels, Mr. Slatten," it said. "I've brought you some!"

"All right, Lizzie. Hang 'em on the rack."

"Yes, sir."

Lizzie entered the room, leaving the door ajar. She shuffled across to the washstand, put the towels on the rack, and made sure that there was water in the pitcher. This particular lodging house did not boast running water.

Slatten winked at Henry Burl.

"Lizzie, you're some girl!" he said. "Always want to be sure a man's comfortable, don't you? You'll make some guy a good wife one of these days!"

"Now, you stop your teasin'," Lizzie said.

Her back was turned to Slatten. He could not see the expression of her face. Had he seen it, he might have had food for thought.

CHAPTER III

DISHONOR AMONG THIEVES

Lizzie Larman never would have attracted notice as a beautiful girl. She was small, faded, her twenty years having the appearance of thirty-five at least. Her dusty-colored hair was stringing down at the sides of her head. She was stoop-shouldered.

Her hands were coarse and red and the nails irregular. Her feet were encased in shoes that were too large for her, the heels of which were run over. Her dress was a combination of "Mother Hubbard" and dressing gown. Her apron had holes in it and was twisted to one side.

She fussed around the washstand, gathering soiled towels, putting the soap into its proper dish, brushing imaginary dust from the corners.

"Lizzie!" said Slatten.

"Sir?"

"You're a great girl, Lizzie!"

"Now, sir—"

"No question about it. I'm liable to go to gettin' stuck on you, Lizzie! I never saw such beauty and such a figger. And you have got the daintiest hands, Lizzie."

"You're foolin'!" she accused. "My hands are red and coarse. Workin' makes them that way."

"Now you're just bein' modest, Lizzie," Slatten said. "No sense in bein' too modest. Ain't she a beauty, Burl?"

"Sure is!" Burl said.

"Lizzie, we're goin' to step out one of these days," Slatten continued. "You're goin' to doll up in your other dress, and maybe we'll take in a show."

"You're teasin'," Lizzie accused again.

"Don't you believe it, Lizzie!"

"I don't like to be teased!" she said. "I know that I ain't pretty. All I get here is not enough to let me dress swell. If I had money, maybe I could fix myself up. Gee, I wish I could!"

There was an expression of longing in her face for a moment. Gus Slatten laughed long and loudly. There was scorn in his laugh, too.

"You poor simp, you couldn't fix up in a million years!" he declared. "You'll always look like you do now. Close the door gently as you go out!"

Lizzie Larman's face flamed, and she sniveled a bit. She hurried from the room, and she slammed the door, too. She went on down the hall and into the little room she called her own. Her work was done for the day.

Sitting on the edge of her cot, Lizzie Larman wept for a moment.

"I suppose it's true," she gasped. "But I'd try. I'll bet I could look as good as some!"

Lizzie Larman, though nobody knew it except herself, had an affair of the heart. She always had been a drudge. In the world of men and women she did not amount to much, and she realized it. She was treated about the same as a cur dog, and she resented it mentally if not physically.

Always compelled to do hard, menial work, she had had no opportunity to enjoy the pleasures of youth. But ambition was not dead within her. And she remembered the evening when, returning io the lodging house after carrying a package to the branch post office for the proprietor, two drunken men had stopped her and indulged in a laugh at her expense.

Lizzie Larman had been unable to do anything. She had stood with her back to a building and wept. And then there had come down the street a prince. He was dressed like an ordinary policeman, but he was a gallant prince so far as Lizzie Larman was concerned.

He grasped the two men who were tormenting her, and he cracked their heads together so that it sobered them. He informed them that he did not want the jail cluttered up with such trash, and so he would not send them in this time. But if ever he saw them in that vicinity again, he would take them in.

The two men had sneaked away, and then the policeman had turned to Lizzie.

"Where do you live, miss?" he had asked.

"I work in the lodgin' house down the street," she had replied.

"I'll walk that far with you. If those men, or any others, ever bother you again, look me up. My name's Renbolt."

"Mine's Lizzie Larman."

For the first time in her life Lizzie found herself with an escort. They walked slowly, for Officer Renbolt was looking for a man wanted at headquarters and must needs glance here and there continually, but to Lizzie the short journey was made with the speed of an express train.

They came to the entrance of the lodging house finally, and Patrolman Renbolt removed his cap and bowed and wished her good night. Then he continued on his beat, and Lizzie Larman dashed up the stairs and to her room, her cheeks flaming. It was an event!

On the following evening Lizzie Larman sat before the front hall window on the second floor for more than an hour, but finally she was rewarded by seeing Patrolman Renbolt pass on the opposite side of the street.

That satisfied her for the time being. She hurried to her cot, admitting to herself that she was in love. And it was a hopeless love, too, she told herself. Why should such a splendid man look at her a second time?

However, being in love, she was bold. She knew what she wanted, and, though she saw no way of getting it, she did not cease to hope. Patrolman Renbolt never knew that the several "accidental" meetings he had with Lizzie Larman were not so accidental as they seemed. And Lizzie never knew that each meeting put her further from her goal, that Renbolt kept telling himself what an uncouth creature she was.

Two things now dominated the life of Lizzie Larman—her unspoken love for Renbolt and her hate for Gus Slatten. The latter had come to the lodging house, and from the first had made it a point to poke ridicule at Lizzie.

Slatten's jests were concerning her personal appearance, and they served to cause her anguish. The more she tried to look presentable, the more she failed. It could not be done without money, and she had little of that.

Lizzie studied the other women she saw. She believed that, did she have money, her hair could be fixed to look like something, and her hands, too. She did not have a bad figure, but how was anybody to know that when she was compelled to wear ill-fitting clothes?

She felt that she should do something to attract the attention of Officer Renbolt. She read the newspapers, particularly the police news, and now and then when she met him "accidentally" she discussed crimes with him. Officer Renbolt smiled at the interest she showed in police work.

But Lizzie was demonstrating what constant application can do. She knew the tricks of policemen, and she knew the tricks of crooks. She was well aware of the fact that some of the lodgers in this particular rooming house were criminals. She was observing.

She had decided some time before that Gus Slatten was a crook, and that Henry Burl was his pal. Once she suspected them of turning a trick and was at the point of speaking to Officer Renbolt about it. But she did not. She was afraid that she had made a mistake, and that Renbolt would laugh.

But her suspicion served to cause her to keep a close watch on Slatten. Her entrance into the room that evening had been for a purpose. She had been listening in the hall outside the door, and she knew that Slatten and Burl were talking in low tones a part of the time, talking of things that perhaps the police would like to know.

In her room, as she prepared for bed, the hot tears were in her eyes.

"I'd like to get that Slatten," she whispered to herself. "I know he's a crook. If I could turn him over to Mr. Renbolt. it would be great. And—if I only had some money and could fix myself up!"

The following morning she heard of the murder and robbery at Belstein's place. Everybody in the district knew old Belstein. He had been there for years, as long as anybody in business. He did not have a very good reputation, but there was something tragic in an old man being slain like that.

Lizzie followed the case with interest. The bronze had been found, of course, and there were fingerprints on it. But they did not tally with any known prints of criminals. Gus Slatten felt a bit of fear when he read about that. He cursed himself for pulling off his gloves as he had done, before he was ready to leave the place.

But the police seemed unable to do anything about the case. Detectives worked and made no headway. The stolen jewels had not been found, had not been offered for sale. They did not even know the number and value of the gems. Belstein's widow could tell them only that he always kept some gems in that little safe which they had found open the night of the crime, after she had called the police when her husband did not return from the store.

Some of Belstein's race took the matter up. A purse was collected, and a reward of one thousand dollars was offered for the capture of the guilty man. The reward spurred the detectives to renewed activities, but nothing came of it.

Gus Slatten had gone to work at the dock, and Burl had a job there now, too. They worked hard, ate regularly at the same place, slept regularly. In common with others in the district, they were watched for some time, and then the watch ceased.

Burl came to Slatten's room now and then in the evening, and Lizzie always tried to listen to what they said. But she could not understand their words. She continued hating Slatten and adoring Patrolman Renbolt.

One month after the crime, Burl paid his customary visit to Slatten's room.

"Well, over your scare?" Slatten asked. "The cops haven't done much, have they? They are thinkin' that whoever did it made a get-away and left town."

"I get scared at times," said Burl. "Slatten, maybe we'd better sell those gems and beat it. I don't like to hang around here. I'd feel safer if I was in some other town."

"We'd better wait," said Slatten. "The cops may be keeping an eye on us, for all we know. That fellow Renbolt talks to me whenever we meet."

"He ain't a detective—only a patrolman," Burl replied.

"I'm glad to see that you've got sense enough to understand that," said Slatten. "I was wonderin' whether what I said would throw a scare into you. Sometimes you've got a flash of nerve. Burl, and sometimes you haven't."

"It's all right to have nerve, but there's no sense in loafin' around here and waitin' to be picked up," Burl said.

"I think we'd better take it easy for another month. Then we can drift. We can start talkin' about it now—tellin' the boys we work with that we're savin' money and intendin' to go West."

"All right!" Burl said.

After he had departed, Slatten began considering things. He knew that the diamonds were worth a great deal of money, even the way he would be compelled to sell them. And half of that money would go to Burl.

Was there any sense in that? Was there any sense in this honor-among-thieves stuff? There was not, the way Slatten could see it now!

He decided that it would be the thing to double-cross Burl and take it all. It would not be at all difficult to do. He could sell a few of the gems at once and make his get-away. And he could sell the others after he got out of town. Burl never would find him. And Burl would never dare open his mouth about it, either!

Since putting the stones beneath the floor, Slatten had not looked at them. He wanted to look at them now. He got up and put a towel over the keyhole, drew down the window shade, and crawled beneath the bed. With a chisel he pried up the end of the board.

He put his hand into the hole and drew out the little bag. Opening it, he counted the stones again and gloated over them. He would be a fool to give Burl half the proceeds, he decided. Burl—what was on his conscience, anyway?

Returning the bag, he pressed the board into place. And then he began singing again, and as he sang he drove the nails home. He looked at the work, smeared dust over the board and the nails, and got up.

There came a timid knock at the door.

Slatten crossed the room swiftly, unlocked the door, and opened it. Lizzie Larman stood there.

"I—I forgot your clean towels," she said.

"Confound it, you're a pest!" Slatten exclaimed. "I wish that you'd always put them towels on the rack before I get home. You come prowlin' around here and botherin' me when I want to spend a quiet evening alone!"

"I—I'm sorry," Lizzie said.

She grinned at him and put the towels on the rack and then crossed swiftly to the door again. After she had left the room. Slatten slammed the door and locked it once more. He picked up from the floor the towel he had had draped over the keyhole and tossed it onto the washstand.

"Silly little fool!" he growled.

Down beside the table he sat, to roll a cigarette and puff at it and consider the matter. He decided that he would sell a couple of the stones, make his getaway, and leave Burl behind. He could do it without Burl knowing. He could leave the following payday. And Burl would not dare talk about it!

"Give half to Burl? I guess not!" Slatten told himself.

CHAPTER IV

LIZZIE GETS BUSY

Lizzie Larman's course in crime detection, gained through the newspapers and magazines, stood her in good stead now.

Lizzie Larman had natural intelligence and adaptability, though few would have suspected it. All that she needed was the chance to apply herself and the reason for doing so. And she had the chance now, and two reasons—her love for Patrolman Renbolt and her hatred of Gus Slatten.

Stepping from the room, Lizzie hurried to her own. She sat down on the side of her cot and gave herself up to thought. She had noticed several significant things.

Gus Slatten, she knew, had been on the floor and probably beneath the bed. He had taken a little longer than usual to get to the door, and there had been dust on the front of his trousers. None knew better than Lizzie that there was dust beneath the bed.

Also, he had had a towel over the keyhole. She had tried to look through the keyhole before knocking and had not been able to do so, and when he opened the door, the towel had dropped to the floor, and she had seen it there.

Lizzie felt sure that Slatten was a criminal, that he had committed some crime recently. It came to her mind that if she collected the evidence to prove him guilty and turned it over to Patrolman Renbolt he would get credit from his superiors, and possibly he would look upon Lizzie Larman with greater favor.

The thought made her almost dizzy. She allowed her mind to dwell upon it. She got up earlier than usual the following morning, got some of her work done earlier, and in the middle of the forenoon, when she knew that Slatten was safe at work at the dock, she went to his room, locked the door, and began her investigation.

Getting down on her hands and knees, she inspected the floor along the side of the bed next to the wall. She could tell at a glance that Slatten or somebody had been stretched there.

The board was nailed in place, but Slatten had not been careful about it. A tiny splinter had been split from the side. Lizzie Larman guessed that there might be something beneath the board. But she feared to tear it up at the moment. The proprietor of the lodging house might call her. She would do that later.

For the remainder of the day she thought about it. But she did not want to make a mistake, and so allow herself to appear ridiculous in the eyes of Patrolman Renbolt. Lizzie Larman wanted to be sure of her ground.

That evening she descended to the street level and loitered around the entrance until she saw Patrolman Renbolt approaching. She walked down the street slowly, so that they would meet near the corner.

Officer Renbolt greeted her cordially, as he would have greeted any one of a thousand persons he met on his beat.

"I—I'd like to tell you somethin'," Lizzie said.

They started slowly down the side street, where there were few pedestrians.

"I'll bet we've got crooks in our lodgin' house," she said.

"It wouldn't surprise me any," Renbolt told her.

"I—I've got an idea."

And what is that?"

"I could get you fingerprints," she said.

"How do you mean?"

"I could get finger prints of every man there. And you could take them to headquarters and have them examined. Maybe you'd find a crook somebody wanted."

Officer Renbolt chuckled. “That isn’t exactly in my line,” he said. “The detectives attend to those things. The fingerprint man would chase me out if I went into his office with a lot of prints like that. It takes time to examine fingerprints.”

“I—I didn’t know,” she said. “But—they found fingerprints on that piece of bronze that killed old Belstein, didn’t they?”

“Yes.”

“And they weren’t prints of any regular crook?”

“Not so far as could be learned,” Renbolt said.

“Now suppose I got some prints that would be like those?”

“In that case we’d make it interesting for some fellow,” said the officer.

“I—I got an idea, but maybe you’ll laugh at me.”

“Certainly I’ll not laugh at you, Lizzie.”

“There’s one of our roomers actin’ funny. I think that he’s a crook, even if he is pretendin’ to work some place. I won’t tell you anything about it now, ’cause it might be a mistake. But if you’d just let me give you his prints— just that one man’s—maybe you’d find he was a crook or had killed Belstein.”

Patrolman Renbolt looked at her sharply. Possibly this girl knew something, he thought. And he was eager to do something to gain promotion for himself. If he could turn up some big crook in hiding, might he not get a sergeantcy?

“All right, Lizzie!” he said. “I’ll take a chance on the finger-print expert throwing me out. I’ll take this man’s prints, whoever he is, and have them examined. Can you give them to me tomorrow night?”

“Sure,” she replied.

Lizzie Larman hurried back to the lodging house. She ascertained that Slatten was not in his room. She polished a drinking glass as well as she could, carried it carefully in a towel, and put it on Slatten’s washstand in place of the one then there. She filled his water pitcher, also the little pitcher that held drinking water. And she managed to finish just as Slatten returned to the room.

“I’m just goin’,” she said.

“Always hangin’ around,” Slatten growled. “Why don’t you do your work in the daytime?”

“Yes, if I did you wouldn’t have fresh water to drink,” she told him. “I just put fresh drinkin’ water in here so you could have a good drink before you went to bed. I reckon I won’t bother about it again.”

“Don’t get huffy over it,” Slatten advised her.

It happened that he wanted a drink. As Lizzie Larman crossed the room toward the door, he picked up the glass, poured it full of water, and drank. Out in the hall. Lizzie Larman exulted.

She had no idea that Gus Slatten was guilty of the murder of old Belstein. She had intimated that just to get Officer Renbolt to take the fingerprints. What she did hope was that they would find that Slatten was a crook, or that he would do something crooked later and leave his prints and so meet with disaster. She wanted to get Slatten out of the way because of his treatment of her, and she wanted Officer Renbolt to get credit for the arrest.

As soon as Slatten left for work the following morning, she hurried to his room and wrapped the glass carefully in a clean towel, substituting another glass for it. She put the glass in her own room and went about her work.

She was kept busy that day and did not have a chance to look beneath the floor of Slatten's room. She did not believe that she would find anything there, but something seemed to urge her to make a search.

Evening came, and, her labor done, Lizzie Larman watched for Patrolman Renbolt again. She had wrapped the towel-covered glass in a piece of paper and had made a neat bundle of it. When she saw him walking down the street, she hurried to meet him. and around the corner she handed him the package.

"It's a tumbler," she said. "I polished it and then watched him use it. Nobody has touched it except that one man. If—if it's any good, I'll tell you who he is. And I'm watchin' him, too, and watchin' somethin' in his room."

"All right, Lizzie! I'll have it examined and let you know the result," Renbolt said.

Her heart fluttering, she hurried back to the lodging house and went to her room. Officer Renbolt looked after her and smiled. There were some queer persons in the world, he told himself.

But he would be honest with her. He would have the fingerprints examined and tell the finger-print man some wild tale to account for it. After all, a man never could tell. Perhaps Lizzie Larman knew what she was doing.

He decided that he would turn in the glass the first thing in the morning. It would cost him an hour of sleep, but he could afford that. And so Patrolman Renbolt went on down the street attending to his police business and thinking nothing more of the affair.

CHAPTER V
MAKING A DATE

When she got off her cot the following morning, Lizzie Larman had a moment of fright. She wondered whether she had acted the fool.

Suppose Patrolman Renbolt met her that evening and smiled and told her that the fingerprints meant nothing so far as the police were concerned? Would he not think that Lizzie was a little silly who should be attending to her own business instead of bothering hard-working policemen?

She trembled a bit and felt despondent when she thought of the possibility of that. But she began her work and watched carefully to see when Gus Slatten left for the dock. She intended to examine his room this day. The proprietor of the lodging house would be gone all morning, and she could work without fear of interruption.

But it was almost noon before she got the chance to begin her investigation. Her work seemed to be delayed that morning by trivial things. And when at last she was able to disappear for a time, she got a hammer and a small chisel, went to Slatten's room, and slipped inside.

She put hammer and chisel beneath the bed and started making up the room as usual. She worked swiftly, dusting and cleaning after a fashion, making the bed, filling the water pitcher again. And she was so eager and in such haste that she neglected to lock the door the last time she entered.

At length she pushed the bed a couple of feet more from the wall and began prying up the board. Now and then she stopped to listen, but she heard nothing save the voices of pedestrians in the alley below.

After a time, she had one end of the short board loose. She was careful not to split it as she worked to free the other end. Her heart was hammering at her ribs, and her breath was coming in little gasps. She felt like a burglar. But she remembered Patrolman Renbolt and took courage.

The board came free. Lizzie Larman put her hand down into the hole and felt the bag. She pulled it forth and blinked her eyes as she looked at it. She shook it beside her ear, felt of it, and after a time decided to untie it.

Sitting on the floor, she took off the string with which Gus Slatten had fastened the mouth of the bag. She emptied the contents into her lap—and gasped.

Diamonds! And two keys! The stones seemed to flash at her in the fitful light behind the bed. It came to her mind that here was loot belonging to Gus Slatten, stolen property he had cached away. Here was news for Patrolman Renbolt! Possibly Renbolt would know where the diamonds had been stolen.

It flashed into her mind, too, that she could appropriate the stones, nail the board in place, and profit herself at some future day. But she did not encourage that for an instant. Lizzie Larman was not a thief. Here was a chance for money, and with money she could beautify herself. She wanted money, but not that sort.

"Gee!" she gasped. "I'll bet they're worth thousands!"

She began putting the stones back into the bag, one at a time, looking at each lovingly.

This was payday for Gus Slatten. It also was the day upon which he expected to make his get-away and leave Burl behind profitless. He already had sold two of the smaller stones for enough to take him to another city and allow him to live in style until he felt it safe to sell the remainder.

He drew his money at noon with Burl, ate his lunch, and then went back to work. Burl was working on one side of the dock and Slatten on the other. Slatten knew that he could get away without being seen by Burl.

For half an hour or so he worked, and then he hurried around the corner and sought the foreman.

"I've got to take the afternoon off, boss," he said. "A boy just brought me word that my sister's been hurt."

"All right, Slatten," the foreman replied. "Let me know if you can't come in the morning."

Slatten hurried away. At the end of the dock, he came face to face with Burl.

"Where you goin'?" Burl asked.

"Errand for the foreman," Slatten replied. "If I don't see you again, Burl, don't forget to come up to the room tonight. I want to talk over things."

He hurried on to the nearest street. The perspiration was standing out on his forehead because of his narrow escape. He caught a car and journeyed toward the lodging house, left the car at a corner, and walked briskly toward his destination.

All his plans were made, and it would not take him long. He would get the stones from beneath the floor, hurry uptown, catch a train that left at three o'clock, get off at a certain small town, and catch a train going toward the South. He had everything planned, and he told himself that there could be no hitch.

Slatten reached the lodging house and hurried up the stairs and to his room. He opened the door and stepped inside.

He saw Lizzie Larman sitting on the floor, and the board up. She was putting diamonds back into the bag.

Slatten slammed the door and locked it. Lizzie Larman, stricken with fear, gulped and gazed at him for a moment and then sprang to her feet.

"So!" Slatten cried. "Little sneak, are you?"

Sudden bravery came to Lizzie then.

"I ain't a thief, anyway!" she said. "And you are! You stole these diamonds. You wouldn't be workin' hard if they really belonged to you and you dared sell them."

Slatten advanced toward her. His mind was working swiftly. He knew that the girl hated him, that she would tell the story of finding the diamonds. Once more the vision of prison flashed before his eyes as it had in the Belstein store, and this time there was an added vision—that of the electric chair.

His mind worked rapidly. He had passed nobody in the hall. There was but one thing to do—choke this girl to death, sneak the body into her own room at the end of the hall, and then get away.

Bending forward, his hands like claws, his eyes flaming, Gus Slatten approached her. She was cringing against the wall now, the bag clutched in her hands.

"Give me that!" Slatten commanded.

She was too frightened to move in reply to his order. He crept closer to her.

"Hand it over!" he growled. "I'll teach you not to go prowlin' around a man's room when he's away from it!"

"You stole 'em!" she gasped.

"Did I? And what was you tryin' to do, eh?"

"I—I just found 'em," she gasped.

"Give me that sack!"

Suddenly he sprang. Lizzie Larman gave a scream that could have been heard down in the busy street. Gus Slatten's wild lurch missed her by an inch. He whirled and was after her again and managed to get between her and the door.

He did not speak again now. There was a murderous light in his eyes. He was like a maniac with but one idea.

Lizzie Larman screamed again. And then he grasped her and pulled her toward him. She dropped the bag and began to kick and bite, and she continued her screeching.

"I'll kill you!" Slatten shouted at her, trying to reach her throat. "Tell, would you?"

She bent back her body, turned her head away. Still, she kicked at him and tried to bite the hand that gripped one of her arms. He whirled her toward a corner, still striving to catch her by the throat. A great fear was upon her now. She knew that he would reach her throat soon. And so she gave vent to a chorus of wild shrieks as she fought to keep Slatten away.

Then her shrieks ended in a gurgle. Gus Slatten had reached her throat at last with one of those strong hands of his.

"Now, you—" he began.

There was a tumult in the hall. Something crashed against the door, but it seemed that Slatten did not realize it. Lizzie Larman felt her strength going. Red flashes were before her eyes. And through the red flashes she seemed to see Patrolman Renbolt.

As a matter of fact, she did see Renbolt. He crashed through the door and was upon Gus Slatten instantly. Two blows, and Slatten was stretched senseless upon the floor. A click, and he was handcuffed. And then Patrolman Renbolt sprang to the girl.

She was on the verge of unconsciousness, but the first sound of his voice was enough to arouse her. Renbolt helped her to her feet and to the bed. She looked up at him and tried to smile.

"That—sack," she gasped. "I found it—under the floor. Diamonds! He'd—stolen them. And he came in and—and tried to kill me."

Patrolman Renbolt looked at the sack. "Old Belstein's, or I'm a goat!" he said. "Listen, Lizzie, and answer me quick! Those finger prints on the glass—remember? They got me out of bed less than an hour ago about them. They were the same as the prints on that piece of bronze. Whose prints are they, Lizzie? The man who made those fingerprints killed Belstein."

"They're his," she said, pointing to Slatten.

"Great Scott! Girl, you've landed the man the whole department has been after for weeks. And there's a thousand reward! You'll get that, girl!"

"No—you!"

"I'll get promotion, and that'll be enough for me. You take that reward, and you won't have to work in a place like this anymore. I'll see that you get it. I owe my success in this case to you."

There came a growl from Slatten, now returned to consciousness, but dazed. Patrolman Renbolt hurried over to him.

"Get up and come along, Slatten," he said. "You're going to the chair for killing Belstein!"

"Did—did Burl squeal?" Slatten gasped.

"Ha! So, Burl was in it, was he? Thanks!" said Patrolman Renbolt.

One month later Patrolman Renbolt, walking his beat, heard his name called gently.

"Oh, Mr. Renbolt!"

Patrolman Renbolt whirled around and beheld a vision of femininity. He did not know the girl at first, but a second glance convinced him.

"Lizzie!" he gasped, taking her hand. "Where have you been? And how fine you look!"

"I got me a room uptown and bought some clothes," she said. "And I got busy with hairdressers and manicures and all them kind of people. I never had a chance before."

Officer Renbolt, who was to be Sergeant Renbolt within a few days and knew it, smiled and gulped. This was not the old Lizzie Larman. Her eyes sparkled, and she had a dimple. And the way she carried her well-fitting dress!

"I'm sure glad to see you, Lizzie!" he said. "The trial comes up next week, you know, and you'll be a witness. But I think Slatten will confess and save us that trouble. Burl has confessed already, you know."

"Yes. I read it in the papers."

"And—say, Lizzie."

"Well?"

"Beginning with the first of the month, I'm to be a sergeant."

"Oh, I'm glad!"

"And I'll probably have day duty, then. That leaves my evenings free."

"Uh-huh!"

"How about a supper and a show some evening, just by way of celebration?" Renbolt asked eagerly.

Lizzie looked into the future just as Renbolt finished the sentence, and she smiled dazzlingly.

"Any time, Mr. Renbolt!" she said. "Get out your pencil, and I'll give you my telephone number!"

Johnston McCulley, creator of Zorro, Black Star, The Spider, and several other well-known pulp characters, was a prolific writer who authored fifty novels, hundreds of short stories, and numerous screenplays for film and television, often using pseudonyms for his novels. "Love and Loot" first appeared in the January 28, 1922, issue of *Detective Story Magazine.*

Made in United States
North Haven, CT
16 September 2022

24208080R00082